CAVE
UNDER
THE
CITY

CAVE UNDER THE CITY

Harry Mazer

A Harper Trophy Book

Harper & Row, Publishers

Library of Congress Cataloging-in-Publication Data
Mazer, Harry.
   Cave Under the City

   Summary: With their mother in the hospital and their
father's whereabouts unknown, two boys take to the
streets of New York to escape being sent to a children's
shelter.
   [1. Survival—Fiction.   2. New York, N.Y.—Fiction.
3. Brothers—Fiction]   I. Title.
PZ7.M47397Cav 1986   [Fic]   86-45008
ISBN 0-690-04557-3
ISBN 0-690-04559-X (lib. bdg.)

  (A Harper Trophy book)
ISBN 0-06-440303-3 (pbk.)

Published in hardcover by Thomas Y. Crowell, New York.
First Harper Trophy edition, 1989.

For my brother, my father, and my son

CAVE
UNDER
THE
CITY

1

Ask me something. There's nothing I don't know about this city. I've lived here all my life. You want to go to Brooklyn? You want to go downtown? You want to go to the Roxy? Yankee Stadium? Ebbets Field? The New York Coliseum? You want to go to the Bronx Zoo? It's the biggest zoo in the world. I practically live there.

Where do I live? The Coops. No, not the chicken coops. It's really the Workers Co-operative Colony. Two whole blocks of apartment houses. We live in the first block, in apartment W–42. That means we live in section W, on the fourth floor, apartment 2. Every section has a different letter. The Chrissmans live across the hall in W–41. They've got two boys like we do. Murray and Max Chrissman. Max is way older than I am, but Murray is sort of my friend. Mostly we have our own friends, but on rainy days we horse around a lot on the stairs, and in the downstairs hall that leads to sections X and Y. There's a section Z, too.

Once Murray and I were just fooling around, dueling with a couple of kitchen knives, and I stuck a knife in Murray's back. That sounds worse than it was. Of course it's easy for me to talk. It wasn't my back. But I didn't really stab him, not all the way in. I just sort of stabbed him. You know how you do, acting like you're going to go right through, but holding back all the time. Somehow the tip of the knife got a little bit of blood on it.

I got scared though. He kept trying to see his back. "It's nothing," I said. "I just scratched you." He ran into his apartment, and I just stood there waiting for his mother to come out and murder me.

My mother doesn't like Mrs. Chrissman because she's always after me or my brother for one thing or another. But then my mother doesn't like any woman who doesn't go to work or isn't active outside the house. She says Mrs. Chrissman isn't an interesting person to talk to. My mother should have heard Mrs. Chrissman that day. She would have learned a couple of new words for sure.

After that, whenever Murray saw me he used to brag, "That's Tolley Holtz, the kid who stabbed me in the back."

He made me sound a lot tougher than I am. With my own friends I'm pretty relaxed, but we're not a

2

gang. I hate gangs. Once a gang came down from Barker Avenue to our neighborhood, carrying banana stalks and looking for a fight. I yelled to Bubber to get in the house. He got away, but they grabbed me. I was pushed, they tripped me, and I went down. I was on my back in the gutter and they were standing over me swinging these banana stalks. Bubber yelled, "Leave my brother alone." He charged right in on them. It was like David and Goliath. He was a peanut; they could have murdered us, but instead they started laughing and we got away.

My gang, four of us, more or less, hang around together. We're not a sports gang. We're sure not a hitting gang. More a talking gang, because that's what we do best. We talk about everything. We talk about sports and politics, the New York Yankees and Lou Gehrig, and what President Roosevelt is doing about the Depression. We talk about music and about the kidnapping of the Lindbergh baby. The Lindbergh case is in the paper every day.

The police have arrested Bruno Hauptmann, an unemployed housepainter from the Bronx. They say he did it. Hauptmann is a painter, like my father. Lindbergh is a flying ace—so who are they going to believe? The police traced a ladder they found leaning against the Lindbergh house in New Jersey. They say Hauptmann went up to the second floor and took the baby, but left the ladder. That's pretty stupid.

"I hope they make him fry," George said, smacking his lips. "Zzzzzzz, like an omelet."

Chick was laughing like a hyena. The only thing he cares about is his music. He plays the clarinet.

"How would you like to fry?" I said to George. "You know what it feels like?" Anything George says, I disagree with.

"Just turn me over easy."

"You'd make a good cannibal," Irv said. "What if the guy's innocent? My father said they're framing a poor workingman."

"What frame-up? What are you talking about?" George's father is a cop. One of his uncles is a detective. "The cops don't frame people up. They get evidence, hard facts. What do you know?"

"Do you know what you're talking about?" Irv said. "You open your mouth and hot air comes out. Do you know anything about the labor movement in this country? The class struggle? Did you ever hear of Sacco and Vanzetti?"

"That's a lot of commie crap."

That's pretty typical of us. We play handball, too, and we throw a football around. We're okay, but we're not the best. When they're choosing sides for stickball, Murray Chrissman is the first one picked. He's the best hitter in the Coops. He hit a ball once from one end of Britton Street to the other. I'm no hitter at all. I throw the ball pretty good, but I can't hit.

I know I could be a better hitter if I didn't have to think about my brother all the time. My mother works, and I have to keep an eye out for Bubber after school and make sure he gets home all right. In school they call him Robert, but everywhere else he's Bubber. Bubby . . . Bubele. Baby, that's what it means. He's sure a baby around my mother. The minute she sits down, he's on her lap. My father says it's because she left him when he was six months old to go back to work. But my mother had to do it because my father wasn't working much. He still doesn't work much.

My father's a housepainter, and he also hangs wallpaper and does floors. But hardly anyone wants their houses painted anymore because there's no money. My father plays cards a lot with his painter buddies. My father's not the only one out of work. They're calling it hard times. Irv's father says it's the worst depression this country has ever had. He hasn't worked for two years. George's father is working. Cops always have a job. Chick doesn't have a father. His mother makes women's hats.

Every day, on my way to school or after school, I see men on the street or in the park, sleeping on newspapers, or down by the railroad tracks past the river. If you're smart, you don't go down there alone. I think a lot about living outdoors. Sometimes I think we could live in a cave by Orchard Beach, and have a fire and fish off the rocks, but mostly I think we're lucky my mother has a job.

My mother works in a dress factory down around 135th Street. I've been there lots of times. It's over a row of stores, a big loft with a lot of women, and men, too, cutting and pressing and working at sewing machines. My mother wanted to take my father up there and teach him how to be an operator on dresses, but he said it wasn't work for a man. I wouldn't want to work there, either. The place is full of thread and dust. It's piecework—every piece has a price—so you have to work fast. My mother is one of the fastest workers.

My mother worries about Bubber a lot. She doesn't worry about me. Bubber doesn't do too good in school. He can't read and he's not learning. The minute the teacher stops standing over him, he's looking out the window or walking around. I'm supposed to help him because I'm older and I'm good in school. My mother can't do it because she works and she has the house and her English isn't that good.

I tell Bubber a word ten times, and then when he comes to it in the book it's always: "What's that word, Tolley? Tell me again."

"Was."

"Was," he repeats. Big smile. He's got a nice smile. That's the trouble. He could be mayor of New York with that smile. "I know it," he says.

"Then why'd you ask me?"

"I just forgot."

But the next time he sees the word he forgets it again or says it backward. "Saw," he says, instead of "was." My brother's not dumb. He's good in arithmetic. Sometimes I think he does it just to keep me sitting there. I stay with him till I can't stand it anymore, then I bop him one. He runs and tells on me, and I'm the one who gets the dirty looks and has to hear how hard my mother works and I'm the oldest and she's getting no help from me at all.

2

Why does Bubber have to do everything I do? Why does he follow me around? Play my games? I have to tell him wait, wait. You'll get a turn. But he can't wait. He has no patience for anything. He gets the ball and he does something crazy, runs away with it. If I grab it from him, he tries to bite me. Then he disappears.

I'm supposed to find him. "Where's your brother?" That's what I hear all the time. "Where's Bubby? You're supposed to be taking care of him. Where'd you leave him?"

Bubber is scared of the cellars, and he's too little to open the doors to the roofs. He likes to sit under the hall stairs, or between the rocks in the empty lots across the street. If he's not there I look by the candy store. After that, if he isn't on the street, I don't know where to look. I start to get scared. He could walk off with anyone. Somebody puts out their hand, he'll walk away with them. He's that kind of kid, cute, with curly hair and a big smile. It could be another kidnapping story. Another Lindbergh-baby case.

Once I went looking for my brother and I couldn't find him anywhere. He wasn't by the rocks or on the street or by the candy store. I didn't know where to look anymore, and I didn't dare go home without him. I looked for him all the way up Allerton Avenue, past the elevated train tracks and the closed-up summer movie house, which is just like a regular theater, with seats and a screen, except there's no roof.

I went past a vegetable and fruit stand where the man was singing out to the people walking by. "I got onions big as apples and apples like grapefruits and grapefruits like honeydew melons. I got tomatoes, potatoes . . ." It was the kind of place my brother would like, but he wasn't there. There was a delicatessen nearby with long cheeses hanging in the window, and strings of mushrooms and garlic, and sacks of nuts in the doorway and candies in silver papers. Bubber wasn't there either.

I was all the way up by the Italian church with the stone grotto around the side. Bubber likes to stand there and look at the waterfall. I saw a gang I didn't recognize, so I crossed over and went home on the other side of the street, checking the Allerton Theater and the ice-cream parlor and Saperstein's Bakery.

By our house I crossed back over and looked up at our lighted windows. What was I going to tell my mother? I was sure my brother was gone. Lost. Someone had stolen him.

I dragged up the stairs, stopping at every floor. I was remembering all the good times I used to have with my brother, all the times I played with him or read the comics to him (*Krazy Kat* was his favorite. His second favorite was *Little Orphan Annie*). Sometimes we'd make believe the rubber tree in the corner of the living room was an apartment house, and the branches were different floors and the little pipe-cleaner people we made were the tenants. I didn't play like that in front of my friends, because it was baby stuff, but I still liked to do it with my brother.

"You're finally home?" my mother said when I came in.

"I went all the way to Boston Road."

"What were you doing there?"

"I can't find Bubby." I was close to tears.

"Bubby is in the toilet. He came home right after you left."

I fell down on the floor. I went mad. I kicked the floor, pounded it with my fists.

"Stop it," my mother said. "They'll hear you downstairs. Come here, come here. Let me take you around." She pulled me up and put her arms around me. "Foolish boy, what are you so upset for? He's home. Your brother is home. Stop crying. What's wrong? Everything's all right."

3

Something's wrong in my house. My father comes in and goes out. He doesn't stay home anymore. My mother is tired all the time and she yells a lot. My father doesn't yell that much. Mostly he just looks at you and shakes his head, and that's as bad as anything.

My mother is always tired. The place she works in is a sweatshop. All day my father hangs around at the union hall with his painter friends. Then my mother comes home and nothing's done and they fight.

I can't stand it when my parents fight. I don't want to hear it. I put my hands over my ears. I want to run out. I want to go to the toilet and lock the door. I look at the shades on the window. One's up, one's down. The closet door is open. It looks crazy to me. I hear their voices, on and on, like the bird house in the zoo. I want to run out.

I get between them. "Okay, cut it out, cut it out. Shut up! Don't fight, please."

My mother is coughing, spitting into a napkin. Her face is white. There's black under her eyes. Her hair is black like wire. She sits there staring at the wall, she doesn't move. My father pats her shoulder. I want her to feel better, to get up and do things.

They never used to fight. My mother was always nervous, but not my father. When he worked, nothing bothered him. He was gone before I got up in the morning. At night when he came home, he smelled of turpentine and oil. My mother had supper waiting. Bubber and I would follow my father into the bathroom while he cleaned up. He liked company. My brother stood on the tub and I sat on the toilet. I liked to watch him at the sink in his shorts and undershirt. My father is big, with hair on his shoulders and arms, and bristly black hairs on the back of his hands. He has big, broad feet that look like hands, friendly feet, like a gorilla's feet. If my father grabs you, you know you've been grabbed.

After he soaped himself all over he rinsed, and then he scrubbed and cleaned his fingernails and rubbed his hands raw to get the paint off. "Take a sniff, Bubby. Do I smell?"

My brother would sniff and then I would sniff

to see if the paint smell was gone. My father shaved and put on a shirt and a clean pair of pants. The last thing he did was comb his hair. He rubbed Vitalis into it, then combed it straight back, shiny and flat. Then he went into the other room and hugged my mother.

There are two rooms in our apartment, a main room and a bedroom. The bedroom is where my brother and I used to sleep in the same bed. We slept foot to foot, but we horsed around too much, so now I sleep on a cot in the hall. I can touch the bathroom door and hear the icebox dripping.

My mother worries that the noise we make will disturb the people downstairs. She wants us to sit like statues, not move, not make a sound. Bubber gets yelled at for running up and down too much and sliding on the hall runner, or staying in the toilet too long. "What are you doing in there?" Bubber likes to drop things in the toilet and flush them away. "Is the toilet plugged up?" She rushes in because she's so afraid that water will spill on the floor and get into the apartment downstairs.

The table where we eat and do our homework is in the main room, where my parents sleep. There's a stove against the wall and a sink and cupboards. The icebox is in the hall next to the dumbwaiter. Usually my father eats by himself. My brother and

I are too hungry to wait. My mother never sits down to eat.

My father holds a piece of potato in one hand, a piece of bread in the other. While he eats I do my homework. He cracks the chicken bones with his teeth and sucks out the marrow. When I get my homework done I can go outside. Not my brother. They don't let him out at night by himself, so he never wants me to go.

He hangs on me and begs me to stay home and play with him. He hangs on my leg like a leech. "Let go of me. Let go, Bubber." I whisper it at first, because I'm afraid my mother is going to get nervous. Then I forget and yell. Stupid! Because I give my mother a headache. I do a lot of stupid things, like going out and leaving the lights on in the house. They're always telling me "Electricity costs money." Or when I'm on the street with Bubber, I forget about him or I tease him till he wants to kill me. But that's not the worst. Sometimes I'm really unconscious. Last Halloween I started a fire in the house.

I was having a party with my friends, and I put a paper pumpkin from the five-and-ten in the window with a candle inside. I thought I moved the curtains but I guess not far enough, because they caught fire. I didn't even know it. We were having a pillow fight on my parents' bed when my mother's friend Sylvia walked in. "Boys! Are you blind!" The curtains were burning. "Are you crazy! Don't you see?" She yanked down the curtains and threw them in the bathtub.

I really got it when my mother came home. I knew I was going to get it. My mother started in on me, and when my father came home, he finished it. Bubber dived under the covers. I was too old for that. My father slapped at me, and I kept ducking and trying to slip out of his reach.

"What do you think?" my father said. "You're going to burn the house down."

"Not in the head," my mother yelled. "In *tuchus*." Meaning my behind.

"Say something," my father said. "Talk. Defend yourself. Do you know how old you are? When I was your age I was working."

It's bad to be hit by your father. It's the worst thing. It's worse when you're wrong. Worse because my father never used to hit.

4

I woke up in the night. My covers had slid to the floor. I felt around for them and pulled them back. There was a light in the bathroom. I heard the water in the sink, then the scrape of my father's razor. Why was he shaving in the middle of the night?

The light turned off and he came out quietly, tiptoeing past me. I caught his hand and he bent down. I smelled the witch hazel he used after he shaved. "You're awake," he said. "Good. In a minute I'll come back to talk to you."

I heard my parents talking, their voices like the buzzing of flies. I was drifting off into sleep again when my father sat down next to me. He was wearing his coat and a hat.

I sat up. "Where are you going?"

"Shh. Not far. To Baltimore. I was promised a job. Maybe I'll be in Washington, D.C. You want me to tell President Roosevelt something?"

I held his sleeve, then caught his fingers. My hands wanted to keep him there.

"I want you to help your mother and look after your brother. Don't fight. You're the oldest. You have to be responsible. You're the man in the house now. I'm counting on you, Tolley." He rubbed my head. "You want a kiss good-bye, or do we shake hands like men?"

We shook hands. His suitcase was by the door with his paintbrushes wrapped in newspaper and tied together with string. The hat made him look like he was gone already. I dug my face into his coat, into the rough, familiar smell of paint and dust.

My father patted my back. I hung on him. It was dark and I was scared. What if he got hurt or lost and didn't come back. I didn't want to let go. "A good boy. A good boy." My father squeezed me, then he pulled away and I had to let him go.

I closed my eyes. I didn't want to see him leave. I heard the door shut. Then his steps disappearing down the stairs. From the main room I heard my mother coughing.

In the morning my mother was fixing breakfast. I got the milk and the butter from the icebox in the hall. Only a sliver of ice remained. I emptied the tray underneath. "We need ice," I said.

"You'll have to wait for the iceman. Squeeze some oranges."

I sliced the oranges, then squeezed the juice. Bubber's juice had to be strained. He was standing by the window in the other room, playing with a shoe. "Get dressed," I told him. Then I went to the toilet.

He was still playing when I came back. I pulled him away from the window. He started to fight me, so I took the shoe away and hit him in the head a couple of times. "Get dressed." He kicked me in the shin. I was going to really crown him; then I remembered what my father had said.

My mother left me a quarter for the iceman. She took my brother with her when she left for work. Bubber was dropped off at a neighbor's who took him to school every morning with her daughter, then brought them back to her house for lunch.

I looked out in the street. A car passed. Model A. Then a '32 Dodge. A LaSalle. I couldn't guess the year. People were going to the train. How was my father going to Baltimore? By train? Was he driving with someone? Was he out of the city already?

A milk wagon stopped across the street. The milkman jumped out, put a feed bag on the horse, then disappeared into a building with a tray of bottles. I saw my friend George and opened the window. "Hey, George, come on up."

"I can't. I have to bring my mother bread so she can make my father's lunch."

I stuck my head farther out the window and watched George disappear around the corner. Across the street I saw a kid standing guard over a pile of stuff—clothes, furniture, a couple of mattresses. "You moving?" I yelled.

He looked up. "Whaaat?"

"Is it your stuff?"

"No, it's my mother's."

I knew what it was. It was an eviction. If you didn't pay your rent you got an eviction notice. Then the marshal came and they carried all your stuff out to the street. I never saw an eviction on our street before. "You're lucky," I yelled. "No school today."

The dumbwaiter buzzer sounded. The iceman was in the cellar. I opened the dumbwaiter door, stuck my head in the shaft, and called down my order. I heard the ice drop on the platform, then the box came up. I unloaded the cake of ice and put it in the icebox. I put the quarter in the box. "Okay," I said, and tugged the rope and the box went down. Then I went to school.

5

After school I waited outside P.S. 96 for my brother. I went across the street and stood on top of the hill. I liked being up on the tops of things and looking way off. Which way was my father? He'd been gone ten days and we'd only received one postcard with his address in Baltimore. The job, he said, wasn't going to last, but he was going to look around. He'd heard there was work in Washington, D.C.

I looked toward downtown. Baltimore was that way, south, past Philadelphia. I looked it up in my geography book, put one finger on New York, my thumb on Baltimore. *Lights out, Pop.* If I had wings and a propeller I'd fly down there like Lindbergh.

Hey, Pop, look up, it's Tolley. How're things going? You get a good job? When are you coming home? You got some good news, I'll tell Momma. She needs something to cheer her up. Pop, you hear me? She's tired all the time and coughing a lot.

"Hey, Irv!" He was down below me in the street. "Piano lesson, today? Do re mi fa . . ." Except for Irv's mother, everyone in his family played an instrument. Me, I played the radio. If I could play something, though, it wouldn't be the violin or the piano. It would be something big like a trombone or a tuba. Some afternoons in the Coops there was music coming out of every single window. It sounded like an orchestra, like the whole house was practicing, everyone trying to drown everyone else out. If I played the tuba, I'd drown them all out.

"Hey, Irv, meet you at the first candy store, later."

Isabelle Arnow looked up. I didn't see her till it was too late. She was going by with one of her friends. Was I screeching? What did I sound like? I thought I sounded like a bird. Not too smart, not too suave. Isabelle! Oh, Isabelle's nice. I don't talk to her, but I look at her a lot. When I'm behind her I look at her neck and the backs of her arms. She has dimples in both elbows. I haven't gotten up the nerve to talk to her yet, but I will one of these days.

I waved to her. Suave, like a movie star, Ronald Colman or Errol Flynn. Isabelle nudged her friend and whispered in her ear. She might have smiled, but she was too far away to tell.

Later, I met my friends at the first candy store. Irv was reading the paper and Chick was shadowboxing with George. Irv's father was on the corner talking to another man. Mr. Horowitz was short, like Irv, with glasses and the same round face. "Hello, Holtz. Where's your father these days?"

"Is this Holtz the painter?" the other man said. "Is your father working? I don't see him around. Where is he?"

"Baltimore."

"Is he working?"

"Who?"

"Am I talking about Rockefeller? I asked you, is your father working?"

"Mmmm."

"You see," the other man said. "That's what I'm telling you, Horowitz. You want to work? A little ambition, that's all that's needed. There's no depression. It's a word the newspapers made up. It's in your head. That's where the fight has to be won. What did President Roosevelt say? We only have to fear—" He turned to me. "What's the rest of it?"

"The only thing we have to fear is fear itself."

"Very good, Holtz. A smart boy. A plus. You see, the schools are doing their part. Now if we all did our parts . . . if everyone believed, had confidence, spent their money. Money, buying, spending, that's what makes work."

"Nothing's going to help," Irv's father said.

"Roosevelt is sticking plasters on a sinking ship. Capitalism is on its last legs." Irv's father talked with both his hands. He was always arguing. "Once the workers in this country unite—"

George grabbed me from behind and dragged me back.

"Hey, you big ape, let go. It's interesting."

He yanked my ear. I gave him an elbow in the gut. Chick, George, and I started to spar around. George had a couple of Baby Ruths. One he ate in front of us. He was a pig. Last summer, Irv and I stopped talking to him completely. We agreed he was a self-centered, egotistical, selfish, ignorant jerk, but when school started we were friends again.

"Who wants some?" George peeled the second candy bar.

Chick took a piece and so did Irv, but I refused. "Eat it yourself, you fat cow."

"Thanks." He stuffed his mouth. "When are you going to treat, Tolley, or are you too cheap? You guys want to go over to Woolworth's and get some jelly beans? Of course, nothing for Tolley."

"If I want anything, I'll get it for myself."

"What are you going to pay for it with? You don't have any money. I heard your family's on relief."

"Hey! You want something, big mouth? You working for a fat lip?"

"You want your head handed to you?"

24

"How'd you like my fist down your throat?"

"How'd you like a pocket full of teeth?" He grinned at me. "So, when are you treating, Holtz? Where's the do-re-mi?" He pushed me. I pushed him back.

Mrs. Russo tapped on the window of the candy store. "Get away from the front of the store! And, you, put the paper down." She slid the small glass window open wider and pointed to the *Daily News* Irv was reading. "Pay for it or put it back. This is not the public library."

"Excuse me, lady." Irv folded the paper, neatly tapping it together, then put it back on top of the pile.

"Two cents and the paper is yours."

"No, thanks," Irv said. "I only read *The New York Times*."

"Nate!" Mrs. Russo bawled for her son. "I've got a few big mouths out here that need to be shut up."

George pawed the ground. "Come on, Nate. Nate! Nate! Come and get us."

We were looking for Nate to come out the door, but instead he came charging around the corner and took us by surprise.

"Chickeeee!" We scattered. But then Chick lost his glasses and he turned back. Nate took a swipe at him. Chick went flat to the sidewalk, then jumped straight back between two parked cars.

"Look out!" A Coca-Cola truck slid up and double-parked behind Chick. "Behind you, Chick!"

He was trapped. It looked like there was only one way out, straight into Nate's hairy arms. Chick didn't hesitate. He dove under the truck and slid out the other side.

Nobody was in our apartment when I got home. Bubber should have been waiting by the stairs. I looked for him downstairs in the hall. "Bubber?" I ran out into the court. "Bubber!" My voice climbed up and down the walls.

"Is that you, Tolman Holtz?" Mrs. Chrissman looked out the window of her apartment. Bubber was with her; Murray, too. "There you are. Come up here." She was waiting for me on the landing. "Where have you been? Your little brother has been sitting here for an hour. The door is locked. He doesn't have a key. He doesn't have a place to go to the toilet. Who's supposed to take care of him? Your poor mother is in the hospital and you're out having a good time."

"My mother is in the hospital?"

"That's right, Mr. Unconscious, a lot you care. She's been walking around with pneumonia. The hospital called me. I had to go down three flights of stairs to the phone. I almost had a heart attack. They took your mother from work in an ambulance. It's in her chest."

I got out my key and opened our door.

"What are you going to do now?" Mrs. Chrissman said. "Wait a minute, I'm still talking to you. Who's going to take care of you?"

"We'll go to my grandmother," I said.

"Good. I was waiting to hear you say it. That's what they said from the hospital. Your mother said you should go to your grandmother. Are you listening to me? I don't want any monkey business. I have enough of my own to think about." She went back to her apartment and shut the door.

6

We climbed the stairs to the train. I had two cents in my pocket, not even enough for one fare. People were coming off the train and the gate was open. I glanced at the man in the change booth. When he wasn't looking we slipped through.

I stood on the platform and watched for the train. Bubber walked around. A woman stopped to talk to him; she opened her purse, and he came back smiling, with a nickel in his hand.

"What did you say to that woman?" I took the nickel from him. "Did you ask her for money?"

"She just gave it to me."

"We don't take money from strangers. How many times did Momma tell you?"

"I didn't take it. The lady gave it to me."

The train came into the station. It made the platform shake. I held on to Bubber's hand. We moved up to the first car, where we stood next to the motorman's booth and watched the tracks merging and dividing, the lights turning from red to green. We rolled past Pelham Parkway station, Bronx Park East, East 180th Street, and then the long, wide, screechy turn by the Coliseum.

We saw the river below, the water spilling out around the icehouse. It was like being on the top of a roller coaster. At Jackson Street the train went down to ground level, past the place where men were loading beef carcasses into trucks. Then the street came up on both sides of us and we were underground. The noise was so bad Bubber put his hands over his ears.

A man sat nearby, wearing a long overcoat. Under his feet there was a heavy metal toolbox. A mechanic, like my father, only my father's tools were paintbrushes and cans of paint and linseed oil.

The train went faster under the ground. The lights flashed by. I thought about being rich and coming home with my pockets full of quarters, taking them out, one at a time, and piling them in front of my mother.

Bubber nudged me. 86th Street. Grandma's station.

The entrance to Grandma's building was like a castle, with heavy wooden doors and long stained-glass windows. Inside, it was dark, and there were big chairs where nobody ever sat, and flags on the walls, and a shield and spears. Bubber stood in the empty fireplace.

We went up three marble steps, then down a narrow corridor. Bubber ran ahead to push the buzzer. We could hear it ring inside. We waited, but my grandmother didn't come.

"Maybe she's asleep. Ring it again."

Bubber gave the bell another jab. She was always here. My grandmother never went out. She always dressed the same way, a kerchief and a wide apron that smelled like cookies. I never saw my grandmother with a coat on. I pushed the buzzer again. Maybe she was getting deaf. I leaned on the door and it swung open.

My grandma's door was never left open. Bubber ran past me. "Buba?" he called. It was dark inside, and there was a smell like something stale. Then Bubber came running out of my grandmother's bedroom.

"Buba's dead."

I went slowly to the room. There was a screeching in my head. I was afraid to look.

My grandmother was lying on her bed. Her mouth was soft and sunken and her nose was like the beak of a bird. Without her kerchief she looked like an old man. Her hands were folded on her breast the way I'd seen dead saints and kings in pictures.

I'd never seen a dead person. I'd seen dead cats

and dead dogs. Dead animals stank and they got bloated. Once I'd seen a dead horse lying on its side in the street. It still had on the straps and harness, and its feet stuck in the air.

"Buba?" Her hand jerked. I jumped back. Sweat popped out all over me. She snorted a couple of times. Bubber was behind me in the hall, breathing like a dog. "Buba's not dead," I said. "She's sleeping."

Her eyes rolled up in her head. "Chillun," she mumbled. She held my hand. Her hand was hot and dry. Bubber climbed up on the bed. She moaned. Her eyes kept closing. "Yuh muddah . . . tell yuh muddah . . ."

"Buba, I thought you were dead," Bubber said.

"Shhh," I said.

My grandmother motioned to her lips. "Wet my lips, child." I ran for a glass of water. She drank it with her hand covering her mouth. She didn't have her teeth in.

"Momma's sick," Bubber began.

I put my hand over his mouth.

"Tell Momma . . . tell yuh muddah . . ." Her eyes closed again.

We went out of the room. Bubber was breathing hard again. "Are we going home now? When's Momma going to be there?"

"I don't know. Leave me alone." How sick was

31

my grandmother? How sick was my mother? How was I going to find my father? I didn't have enough carfare to get home. And I was hungry. I was expecting to eat here. I looked in the icebox and all the cupboards. A lot of pots and empty jars. In a bag I found some old potatoes with skinny white sprouts growing out of them like dead men's fingers. Even the glass cookie jar that always held my grandmother's famous raisin cookies was empty.

In a drawer I found a pencil and paper. "Are you going to write Daddy and tell him Momma is sick?" Bubber said.

"What are you worrying about? Momma is coming home tomorrow and Buba is just tired."

I jabbed black dots across the paper, then joined two dots in the middle. "Your turn." The idea was to keep joining lines and not give the other side a chance to make a box.

"When are we going to eat?" Bubber said.

"When Buba wakes up."

Bubber sniffed. "I smell potatoes." I smelled them, too. Potatoes and onions. My stomach growled.

In the other room I heard my grandmother stirring. I handed Bubber the pencil. "Your turn." I went to see my grandmother. Bubber followed me.

My grandmother was standing by the bed, holding on to the post. Her feet were bare. When she saw me, she covered her mouth and said something

32

that I couldn't understand. "You want me to get you something, Buba?"

She shook her head and went to the bathroom. When she came out she had her teeth in.

"Go home, go home. I told you children to go home. I don't want you to get sick. I have a cold."

"Buba, I'll go shopping for you."

"For what? I don't want anything. I'm not hungry. I just need to rest. Tell Momma I'm just a little tired. I don't want her to come, she has enough. Tell her my neighbor looks in on me. Now, go home. Go home."

I hesitated. I didn't know what to do. I was afraid to tell her my mother was in the hospital. I was afraid I'd make her sicker.

"Go, go," my grandmother said, "what are you waiting for? I'm all right. I told you, take the little one out before he gets sick."

We left. On the way home, I bought two penny candy bars. When we got to the station, I put Bubber's nickel in the slot and pushed him ahead of me under the turnstile.

7

We stayed home from school the next day, ate crackers and cheese, and listened to the radio. I started to write to my father but stopped, because what if my mother came home today, or tomorrow? What if I wrote and he came all the way home from Baltimore and my mother was home already?

The ice had melted and the hamburger that had been sitting on top of it turned brown. It didn't smell too good, but I dumped it into a pan and broke an egg on top of it. Bubber had his nose under my elbow. "Get me salt and pepper. Get the bread."

"The meat is stinky."

"Get the ketchup."

"I won't eat it."

"This is special. Mother Tolley's Deluxe Hash." I stirred the meat grandly with a fork, shook in pepper and salt. My stomach was growling. The pan was too hot and the meat began to smoke. I turned down the fire, then, without thinking, I grabbed the hot handle. I dropped the pan and meat scattered on the floor.

"It's dirty."

"Is it my fault!" My fingers stung like fire. I smeared butter on them. "Go ahead," I yelled, "eat anything you want."

I ran to the bathroom and stuck my hand under the cold water. There was a white line across the palm. I smeared zinc ointment on it, then wrapped a bandage around it. I saw my face in the mirror. I felt mean and ugly. My hair was falling into my mean, squinty eyes. I was sick of being in charge and taking care of Bubber.

Bubber was still by the stove, standing there like I'd whipped him. He was picking at the meat in the sink. I tasted a piece. It had a nice charred taste, like mickies right out of the fire. I spooned everything together in the pan and put it on the table with bread and ketchup. "Okay, let's eat."

Bubber stared at the wall.

"Come on," I said. "Nobody ever yelled at you before? You don't take some, I'll eat it all myself."

He slapped me. "That tickles," I said. He punched me a couple of times hard before he sat down to eat.

"It's good, isn't it?"

He opened his mouth and let me look at the chewed-up meat on his tongue.

For dessert I made chocolate pudding, burned that, too, but Bubber was getting to appreciate my style of cooking. He said it tasted good.

After we ate, I thought about going out. I hadn't seen my friends all day. I looked down into the courtyard. Then I went into the other room and looked out to the street. Back and forth. I'd go out when Bubber was asleep.

At the table, Bubber was drawing and telling himself Tarzan stories. "Now he jumps in the river. Uh-oh, here comes the alligator. But look how fast Tarzan swims. Nobody can swim as fast as Tarzan!"

"Okay," I said. "Stop. Time to go to bed."

"Splash. Splash. Splash. Splash. Tarzan jumps out of the water. I have to do my homework, Tolley."

"What homework? They don't give homework in first grade." He never did anything when my mother was home. Now he wanted to read his book. I had to sit with him and help him sound out the words. Fifteen minutes was enough for me. "Okay, get ready for bed."

No, first we had to play Lone Ranger and Silver. I was Silver. I got down on my hands and knees and he climbed on me. He dug his knees into my sides. We rode to the other room where Tonto was waiting. Then we had to hit the trail after the bad guys. "Hi-ho, Silver!" And the great white horse went galloping to the toilet.

I finally told him, "You want to see Momma tomorrow, you've got to go to bed."

"Is she coming home?"

"She'd better. One more day of you is all I can stand."

I said he could sleep in Momma's bed. I had to get on the bed, too, and we listened to *The Shadow* on the radio. *Who knows what evil lurks in the hearts of men?* It was a good story. Margo was trapped, but the Shadow rescued her. *The Shadow knows. . . .*

Bubber fell asleep listening. He had his feet over me. I was careful getting out of bed. I turned off the radio, carried my shoes to the door and went out.

It was late. There was nobody by the first candy store. Nate was taking in the papers, getting ready to close up. I walked up toward the subway. Most of the stores were shut. The drugstore was open on the next corner. I waited by the delicatessen under the tracks for the next train from downtown. What was I waiting for? I didn't expect my mother, but I stood there and waited.

When the train came into the station, a handful of people got off. A woman came down the stairs. She was wearing a leopard-skin coat and a matching hat. My mother didn't have a coat like that, but there was something about her that made me think of my mother. I started toward her—I was happy. But it was just a woman. After that I went home.

The minute I came off the street and into the courtyard, I heard Bubber crying. He was standing in front of the open window, bawling like a cat. "Momma . . . Momma . . . Momma . . ."

I called up to him. "Shhh!" I didn't want the whole house to hear. "I'm here, shhh. Shut up." I ran up the stairs, fell and banged my knee. Then I had to fumble around for my key because he didn't have the brains to open the door.

"What's the matter with you?" I said, when I finally got in. "What are you broadcasting for? You want everyone to know what a baby you are?" That's what he looked like, a pouty, sticky-eyed baby. "I only went down for a second. I came back, didn't I? What did you wake up for? I heard you all the way out in the street. What are you afraid of? I left the light on."

He burped. It smelled like burned meat.

"I have a right to go downstairs. I don't have to be with you every second. Clam up, will you?" I mixed Ovaltine with water. There was no milk in the house. It tasted terrible and I spilled it down the drain.

Later, I lay in bed. The light came in from the street. Somebody had a radio on. I heard a woman shouting and I thought of my mother, and my grandmother all by herself. Tomorrow, if my mother wasn't here I was going to go to the hospital. My mother would tell me what to do. *Come home*, I'd say. *You can stay in bed, Momma, and give the orders. I'll cook, do the shopping. I'll take care of Bubber, too. Tonight's not a good example, Momma.*

I pulled the blankets over my ears. The last thing I remembered was thinking about breakfast. I'd make oatmeal with raisins and brown sugar.

8

Bubber woke me in the morning. He was sitting on my back singing. "O beautiful for spacious pies, forever waves of rain."

"Off!" I humped up with my feet, then dug my head under the pillow.

"For purple mountains magic ski, above the fruited plates. Amer-i-ca, Amer-i-ca . . ."

We were going to the hospital today.

"Amer-i-ca, Amer-i-ca, God shed his grapes on me."

I got up and checked the door. No milk. Yesterday was the day we were supposed to pay. There were two bottles of milk and a pint of cream in front of the Chrissmans' door. I went back inside and made oatmeal. Bubber picked out the raisins, then ate a couple of spoonfuls. He wanted butter and milk with his cereal. "That's all you're going to get until we see Momma and get some money." He went to his room and came back with four Indian-head pennies.

I found a quarter in the lining of my mother's pocketbook. I went through my father's pants. All I found was lint, but in the handkerchief pocket of his good jacket I found a dollar bill. "Look at this," I said, "a dollar bill!" It was like magic finding it. Great feeling.

We didn't leave the house till the kids had gone to school. There was a man singing in the courtyard, his hat on the sidewalk. I wrapped a penny in newspaper and aimed for the hat. It landed in the bushes, but he found it. Musicians come into the courts all the time, playing for pennies.

We tiptoed down the stairs, but instead of going out on the Barker Avenue side, we went out through the cellar. It was dark and smelled garbagey. A cat leaped out of a can. Bubber held my arm until we came out on the park side.

We walked to Fordham Hospital through the park and the Botanical Gardens. The Gardens' gate was chained shut on our side, but I knew a way in by the pond. Once we were inside, nobody stopped us. A crow hee-hawed and Bubber hee-hawed back.

The hospital was a long red brick building with a lot of skinny windows framed in white. Which window was my mother's? Maybe she'd call down to me, the way she did at home.

There were people going in and out of the hospital. Nobody paid any attention to us. Inside, next to the entrance, was a little newsstand. I'd never been in a hospital before, except when I was born, which I didn't remember. The only other time was when I had my tonsils out. All I remembered about that was how my throat burned and I cried for ice cream.

"What's that?" Bubber said, pointing.

"Don't point. Just look. That's a Jesus Christ."

"Why's he like that? Is he sick?" Bubber made his arms like the Christ.

I glanced at the man behind the news counter. He had white eyes. He was blind. "Don't worry about it," I said, pushing Bubber along.

"Can I help you boys?" The voice came from behind some palms. A strict-looking woman was sitting at a desk.

"I want to see my mother, Mrs. Holtz."

She ran her finger down a long list. "Anna Holtz?"

"Yes, that's my mother."

"Mine, too," Bubber said.

"She's in room 403."

"Okay, thanks." I turned Bubber's head around. He was staring at a legless man in a wheelchair.

"One minute, boys. Wait a minute," the receptionist called after us. "You can't go up there."

Bubber stopped. "Come on," I whispered.

"You, children, stop right there."

Ahead, in front of the elevators, a man in a gray uniform looked our way. "Are you boys a little hard of hearing?"

We went back and the woman pointed to a sign above her desk. "Minors under fifteen not admitted to patient floors."

"I'm sixteen," I said. I stood up straight.

She took off her glasses and looked at me. "You're not sixteen. You're not fifteen. You're not even close."

"No, honest, I really am."

She looked pained. "How old is your brother?"

"He doesn't have to go up with me."

"I can so," Bubber said. "I'm twenty-five." He held up two fingers on one hand and five on the other.

"And how much older is your big brother?"

He held up five fingers.

"I thought so." She smiled at Bubber. Grown-ups always thought Bubber was cute.

"I have to see my mother. It's serious."

"Why?"

"Why? She has to come home. There's nobody at home. We're locked out. I have to get the key from her."

"Why aren't you children in school? Where's your father?"

"Working. He's out of town. That's why I have to talk to her. He left all of a sudden, and he didn't leave any money."

The woman tapped a pencil on the desk. Then she picked up a phone. "Hello, is this the pulmonary ward? This is Mary Byrnes at reception. I have two children downstairs who are here to see—" She looked at the card.

"Anna Holtz," I said.

"Anna Holtz, in room 403. It's their mother. They'd just be coming up for a minute."

She listened, then she shook her head and hung up. "Sorry, boys, I can't let you go up. Your mother is too sick for visitors."

"I've got to see her," I said. "You have to let me go up there."

"Wait a minute now, don't get excited. Maybe I can help you." She picked up the phone again. "Betty? This is Mary Brynes at reception. I have a problem—two children here who need some assistance. Their mother's on the fourth floor . . . pulmonary. Nobody's home with them." She listened. "I know, but they came here—all right . . . yes . . . yes . . . okay." She wrote something down on a slip of paper and handed it to me. It had a name and a room number. "Now you go there and they'll help you out." She pointed to a corridor going the opposite way from the elevators. "Follow that hallway till

44

you come to room fifteen. That's Social Services. They're going to help you."

"Can we see my mother, then?"

"You talk to them first. They'll explain everything. Now, hurry along. They're expecting you." She smiled at me. "Don't worry, they're going to take good care of you."

9

"Seven . . . nine . . . eleven . . ." Bubber was reading the door numbers. "Fifteen. This is it, Tolley."

A gray-haired woman was waiting for us. "The Holtz children? Come right in. I'm Mrs. Winslow."

She seemed nice—she was soft-looking and smiling. We sat down. There was a railing and a gate and desks on the other side. Bubber started counting the rails while Mrs. Winslow went back to talk to a man sitting at a desk. He had a square, doggy face.

"Tolley." Bubber nudged me. "I want a drink."

"Go get it, then. Don't bother me." I was watching Mrs. Winslow, waiting for the chance to tell her how important it was for me to talk to my mother. I had to talk to her and find out if she knew where my father was. If he knew Momma was in the hospital . . .

Mrs. Winslow came back. "Where's the little boy?"

"He wanted a drink. He'll be right back."

"You go in, then. Mr. McKenzie is waiting. I'll get your brother." She held the gate open.

Mr. McKenzie looked at me, then down at some papers. "Sit down, boy." He started asking me questions. "Name? Age? Address?" He glanced up each time, then wrote down the answers. "How long at this address? Parents' names?"

I gave him the wrong address. I didn't do it on purpose, it just came out that way. It was Irv's address, which wasn't too smart, if I was trying to be smart. I don't know why I lied. There were more questions. How long since my father had last worked? Any prior sickness in the family? How long had we been alone? I didn't like all these questions. All I wanted to do was talk to my mother. Five minutes, that's all I needed.

"All right," he said finally. He put down the pen. "There are two of you, aren't there?"

"Mrs. Winslow went to get my brother."

Mr. McKenzie frowned. "He should be here, not roaming the halls."

"I'll get him," I volunteered.

"Stay here. I don't want to lose you, too." He stood up, gathered the papers. "Well, let me go find the driver."

"Are we going up to my mother now?"

He burped and patted his chest. "Let's take care of you and your brother first."

Take care of us? Driver? What was he talking about? "When do I get to see my mother?"

"She can't have visitors. Too sick. I'm sure she'll be relieved to know you're at the children's shelter.

"Thank you, sir." I was on my feet. "Thanks for helping. Thank you very much, sir."

He stopped me at the railing. "Calm down. Everything's going to be all right. You sit right here."

I ran my tongue over my lips. I needed a drink. Where was Bubber?

"Say," he said, "don't look so upset. We're going to take good care of you. Good food, a place to sleep."

You get that in jail, too, I thought.

The minute he went out, I was on my feet. Sweat ran down my sides. The children's shelter! That was for kids in trouble, kids who didn't have families. Maybe they'd put Bubber and me in different places. And if he cried at night, they'd hit him to make him stop.

I nudged the door open. Mrs. Winslow was standing there. "The little boy is with Mr. McKenzie. They'll be here in a minute."

"Bathroom, ma'am. Can I go to the bathroom?" I hopped like I couldn't control myself.

"Down the corridor to your right, Tolley."

48

I disappeared around the corner, down one corridor and up another, looking for Bubber. I didn't know where I was. I thought I heard Bubber crying. My stomach felt all hollowed out. Then I saw them—Mr. McKenzie talking to a man and Bubber standing beside him. The two men started walking toward me. Bubber was behind them.

I hid in an alcove. When they went past me, I grabbed Bubber and we ran for it. Around the corner, past people and wheelchairs and nurses. I pulled Bubber into a little room, just a closet with a sink and mops and buckets.

"Tolley," Bubber said. He was breathing like a dog again.

"Shh!" I put my hand over his mouth. I peeked out—my legs felt like water. I waited till the hall was clear, then we walked out, straight through the main hall, past the newsstand and the Jesus on the wall, and out the door. Across the street, we hopped a bus going crosstown.

The bus was crowded; we wormed our way right into the middle. Mr. McKenzie would forget about us now. There were so many people in the city. Four million people. Why should they care about a couple of kids? Across from us, a woman sat with her arms folded over packages. Another woman read, her lips moving. A man dozed. So many people. Nobody was looking for us. Nobody was looking at a couple of kids. We passed a billboard that advertised a paint that covered the world, blood-red paint spilling over the globe.

I was going to write to my father as soon as I got home. *Come home, Pop, you've got to come home.* I didn't know what else to do. The way things were going was wrong. I couldn't do it myself. *Come home, Pop.* He could go back when my mother came home or my grandmother was able to take care of us.

10

We got off the bus at Pelham Parkway and walked under the elevated train toward Allerton Avenue. Bubber leaned on me and walked with his eyes closed. His shoes were untied and his stockings had sunk down to his ankles. He opened his eyes when we went by the deli. "I'm hungry."

We went in. There was sawdust on the floor and rye bread stacked on the counter. The smell was so good it almost knocked me over. I bought a cream soda and two knockwursts that we loaded up with mustard and sauerkraut. We sat down at a little table by the window.

"Is that a lot of money?" Bubber asked.

"Do you have to know the price of everything?"

"How much?"

"Two times seven cents."

"Fourteen."

"Plus a nickel for the soda."

"Nineteen. Is that a lot of money?"

"What do you think?"

When we went outside, the train passed overhead and Bubber put his hands over his ears and screamed so he wouldn't hear it. He was a funny kid, my brother. Things bothered him that I never even noticed.

He poked along, picking up cigarette wrappers, matchbooks, and Dixie-cup covers. He found a Tom Mix. He had my old Horton-ice-cream-cover collection. It was mostly movie stars. Clark Gable, Wallace Beery and Norma Shearer and Jean Harlow. He had my baseball cards, too, that came with bubble gum. I used to trade them. When I turned twelve, I decided I was too old for them and gave them to Bubber. It was harder to give them away than I thought. I missed them. Sometimes I'd get them from Bubber and put the teams together. The cards still smelled like bubble gum. If I found a card in the street, I'd save it for him. Even if it was a double, he could trade it.

"My feet hurt. Ohhh!" he said, sounding like my mother coming up the stairs after work. "Ohhh, my poor feet."

A trolley car passed and I thought of jumping on the back and taking a free ride, but Bubber would never be able to reach the back window.

We went past our street, over toward Burke Avenue. I didn't want to see anybody I knew. I didn't want anybody to know my mother was sick, and that they were trying to put us in an orphan home.

A couple of blocks from Burke Avenue, there was a block of burned-out stores. Behind the stores, it was all overgrown with weeds and prickly bushes. We poked around for a while. We found an old, soggy mattress with the stuffing coming out, and tires and a wrecked Model A with the doors gone. The seats were gone, too, but Bubber climbed in and stood behind the wheel. "Rrrrrrr." He pushed the horn button. "Beep beep. Come on, Tolley, get in. First stop California."

"What's in California?"

"Daddy?"

"No! That's too far away."

"Alaska."

"Wrong."

"Rrrrrr. There's Daddy." He pushed the horn button again. "Beep beep beeeeep."

Later, before we went home, we stopped at Lazinski's grocery store to buy eggs and some other stuff. "How much butter, Holtz?" Mr. Lazinski had a broad red face, a tomato face, with white eyebrows.

"Quarter pound."

The butter was in a wooden tub in the cooler. Mr. Lazinski cut out a chunk and put it on a piece

53

of waxed paper on the scale. "A little over, okay?"

"And half a quarter of cream cheese." The cream cheese came from the cooler in a long wooden box. I took a box of corn flakes from the shelf, and two cans of applesauce and a package of Wonder bread. Then I added three packages of Drake's cream-filled cupcakes.

Bubber touched everything. "How much? Does that cost a lot?"

I put back one of the cupcakes, while Mr. Lazinski sliced a half pound of bologna and American cheese. I added a jar of mustard and a jar of Heinz pickles.

"All this is yours, then?" Mr. Lazinski added up everything with a pencil on the outside of a paper bag. "Three dollars and fifty cents," he said, snapping open the bag.

"Charge it," I said.

He took the account book from under the counter. He had a page just for us. He looked at the numbers, then pinched his nose. "With today's bill, tell your mother she owes me twenty-nine dollars and twenty-four cents."

That was more than my mother made in a week.

"Tell her I have to have something on the bill. I've already let you charge too much. I have my own bills to pay."

I took the package. "I'll tell her."

In the house, Bubber started eating bread and butter while I wrote to my father. "Dear Pop, You've got to come home right away. Momma's in the hospital and Buba doesn't feel good. We're all right. . . ." I copied the address off his postcard and sealed my letter. I ran out to the candy store and bought two penny stamps to stick on the letter to my father. Then I stood by the mailbox like I was expecting my father to come popping out like Flash Gordon on his rocket ship.

In the house there was no ice, so I put everything in a box on the fire escape. Bubber peeled the paper from a cupcake. He licked out the paper, then he nibbled all around the cake, saving the cream part for last. I sat there and watched him, leaning on my arm the way my father did. I felt like my father, all tired out.

"What are we going to do, Tolley? Are they going to come and take us?"

I turned on the radio and we listened to *Young Widder Brown*. Bubber got bored and played with the doors on the radio, opening and shutting them. The radio was as tall as he was. We both liked *Jack Armstrong, the All-American Boy* and *The Lone Ranger* a lot better.

When the radio program got too boring, we ate. Bubber wanted to know what we were going to do when we ate everything up. The bread was already gone and the bologna. I got mad at him because he kept asking me things I couldn't answer. "Don't bother me," I said, but I went through the house again, looking for money. I felt under the chairs and behind the bed, and under all the plates in the cupboard where they sometimes hid money. I found a nickel and a couple of pennies.

I fell asleep on my parents' bed, listening to the radio. Bubber was asleep already. I had to pull his clothes off and cover him up.

11

In the morning the doorbell woke me. "Holtz?" a man called. "Tolman Holtz, are you in there?"

Then I heard Mrs. Chrissman. She was standing outside our door, too. "The older one told me he was going to his grandmother. If I thought they didn't have anybody, believe me, I would have been the first to take them in."

I signaled Bubber to be quiet.

"He gave us the wrong address," the man said, "then he ran away. I was here yesterday, too, tracking him down."

"Oh, that one, the big one, he's trouble," Mrs. Chrissman said. She banged on the door. "Tolley! Tolley! Are you in there? This is Mrs. Chrissman. Open up."

"I'll look around the neighborhood and come back," the man said. "I'm not leaving without them. If you see them, though—"

57

"Don't worry, I'll hold them for you. They need somebody to control them. Their poor mother. Poor woman. They are a handful. Leave them alone, they're like wild animals."

I heard the man's footsteps going downstairs; then I got up and stood at the window. A tall man in a red plaid jacket and a gray hat came out on the stoop. It was drizzling. He lit a cigarette, stood there for a couple of minutes, then walked away.

Bubber and I got dressed and climbed out on the fire escape. We went up the ladder to the roof and down another set of stairs into another part of the building.

12

It was wet in the park. I found a piece of cardboard and held it over our heads. We came out near the bridge by Gun Hill Road. Under the el we went into an Italian bakery. It was warm inside, and the window was steamed up. I bought a loaf of hot bread and a pineapple tart.

Outside we walked along, ducking into doorways and under store awnings. I passed Bubber hunks of bread. The tart I saved for last. All the time I was thinking about what we would do. We couldn't go back to the house and we couldn't stay on the street all day. Go to Grandma's then. Was she still sick? We'd stay there and help her. But what if the man got Grandma's address, too, and came there and said she was too sick to take care of us and took us away?

Bubber was hanging on to me, trying to hold my

hand. I didn't want him to. It was babyish. "We're okay, aren't we, Tolley?"

"Yeah, great." I kept thinking about the man in the plaid jacket, and there was a tightness in my belly that wouldn't go away.

"I don't want to go to the orphan house," Bubber said.

"Okay." Would it be so bad? At least it was dry there, and they'd feed us.

"Tolley, let's go see Momma. I'm cold. I don't want to stay on the street. I want to go home."

I gave him the heel of the bread. His hair was full of raindrops and he had bread crumbs all over his mouth. I thought of McKenzie, then Mrs. Winslow. She was nice. I'd take Bubber there, room fifteen. I'd let Bubber go in alone, then I'd duck out of there fast. I could take care of myself better alone.

Bubber was crying. He was eating and crying. "What're you crying for?" It made me mad that he was crying. It was like he'd guessed what I was thinking and he was crying because I was going to leave him. And I suddenly saw him kicking McKenzie and trying to run after me.

What would I tell my parents? *Where's your brother?* What would I say? What would I tell my father when he came home? *I don't know. I left him. He went to the orphan home.* What if my parents went for him and he wasn't there? Maybe another family would come and he'd go home with them and nobody would know where he was.

"Come on," I said. I didn't want to think anymore. We followed a woman into a butcher store and stood by the door like we belonged to her. The butcher sharpened a knife, then trimmed a piece of meat, weighed it and wrapped it. When the woman left, we left, too.

Near Burke Avenue a green panel truck slowly turned the corner. It was like the trucks the city used to pick up stray dogs. What if they were picking up stray kids? What if it was the man in the plaid jacket looking for us? We cut behind some buildings, then ducked down into an empty lot. It was a low place, drippy and wet. We were in back of the block of burned-out stores. I looked up at the high foundation walls. We went up an outside staircase to a door. It was boarded up, but a couple of the boards had been pried loose. We slipped inside.

Inside, everything was burned and ripped out. It had been a restaurant, but now it was nothing— holes in the roof and metal ceiling hanging down. The rain dripped through everywhere. It was just a place to be for a while, and we fooled around exploring it.

The floor was wobbly. "Stay on the side," I said.

"You're going to fall through." Bubber was finding things, savers—a cracked dish, a spoon, the handle of a coffee mug that he tried on my finger like a ring.

In front, the checkout counter was smashed and filled with broken glass. In a drawer underneath, Bubber found a book of dry matches. He tried to read the cover. "B— Be— Be—"

"Becker. That's good," I said. "What's this word?" I skipped "restaurant" and went to the next word.

His lips formed. "Hah— ho— hoo . . ."

"Home," I said.

"Don't help me."

"You're taking all week. What's the first word?"

"B— B—"

"Becker's Restaurant. Home-Style Cooking. That's what it says."

"Who cares?" He started lighting matches and throwing them at me. I grabbed the matchbook from him. "Give them back. They're mine."

"You don't play with matches." I put them in my pocket.

In the back there was a hole in the roof over a row of big black stoves. The roof had fallen in and plugged up the stairs. Nearby, there was a dumb-waiter like the one in our apartment, except this one was bigger and the door opened and shut like a mouth. It had a good rope and pulleys. I gave the rope a tug and ran the platform up and down. It was perfect.

Bubber leaned into the shaft and dropped some stones. I got the idea of riding the platform down to the cellar and looking around. Maybe there was still good stuff down there. I climbed on the platform and held myself back with the rope.

"Tolley, don't—"

"Bye, Bubber." I released my grip.

"Tolley—"

I meant to let myself down easy, but I couldn't hold the rope. It slid through my fingers and I hit with a jolt I felt in my teeth.

"Tolley?" I saw my brother's head in the shaft above me. "Tolley, are you all right? Are you dead?"

"Yes, I am dead," I said. I sat there, blowing on my hands and wondering how I was going to get back up again.

13

It was dark in the cellar. No lights, no windows. It smelled like dead cats. I couldn't see anything. I felt around, moving cautiously. Then I heard a scratchy, creaking noise and I saw light. Skinny stabs of light, punching at me in the dark.

Then it was black.

Then the light started again. This time it went on and on. Something cold brushed against my cheeks. I backed toward the elevator shaft. The light exploded around me. It darted and danced and swung around the cellar. I saw a door swinging open.

Then it was black again. Then light. Then black, then light again. The door swung open and shut. I saw a tiny room, a cot and a stove and a broken window.

I looked into the room. It was empty. Whose cot was it? Who lived here? The wind came through the broken window and slammed the door shut. I yanked it open. "Bubber," I called. I ran back to the dumbwaiter. "Bubber, I'm coming up."

I got on the elevator and grabbed the rope, but my hands were too sore to pull. "Bubber, you've got to help me." I kept looking over my shoulder, thinking whoever lived there was somewhere in the dark watching me. "Bubber. Listen. When I pull down on the rope, you hang on and don't let go. If you let go, I'll kill myself."

"I can't."

"You have to." I pulled down the rope as hard as I could and lifted myself a little. "Hang on, Bubber. Hang on." He just had to hold it long enough for me to get another grip, but he couldn't and I fell back. My hands were burning. The cellar was light again. "Bubber, listen to me. Snag the end of the rope over something. Anything. The edge of the frame. Just don't let go."

I wrapped my hands in my shirt and tried again. "Snag it," I yelled, and got another grip. I went up. "Once more." I got my arm over the edge and hung on. Bubber grabbed my shirt and pulled me out. I blew on my hands. I felt the blisters coming. "Good boy," I said.

14

I was afraid to go back to the apartment. For a while we watched a baseball game at the high school. There was a crowd in the stands. Bubber poked around, picking up candy papers and sniffing them. I didn't say anything till I saw him licking the papers. Then I made him stop because it looked so queer.

We hung around the stores, looking at food in the windows. It's the worst thing you can do when you're hungry. All those cakes and bread and apple strudels. Bubber pestered me to buy something. "What am I going to buy it with?" I had three cents in my pocket. We went into a candy store and I bought three pretzel sticks and divided them. Then I asked the man for a glass of water.

I drank half and passed it to Bubber. "Can I have more, please?" Bubber said.

The man filled the glass. "That's it. First water on the house. Next time, a penny a glass."

In a butcher shop, meat hung in the window. I wished I could go to Dave, the butcher on our street, and buy lamb chops. Dave the butcher was young. His hair fell in his face and he had gold teeth. "For you," he'd say to my mother when he brought out a piece of meat. "This is just for you, beautiful. A beautiful piece of meat." Then he'd wink at me. "Am I right?"

I remembered the smell in the house when my mother seared the meat in the pot, then added onions and potatoes and carrots and stewed it slowly. And the good feeling of fat and meat in my belly.

A woman in a dark coat came out of a store. "Carry your bundles, lady?"

She pushed two heavy grocery bags into my arms and marched off. She lived three blocks from the store, on the second floor. By the time she unlocked the door, my arms felt like they were falling off. I set the bags down on the kitchen table. Something good was cooking. Everything in the apartment was clean and warm.

She tied on an apron, looked at the bags on the table, and then gave me a dime. "Is that your little brother?" Bubber was just standing there. "You want a dime, too? Give me a smile," she said. He smiled at her. "What a sweet little boy." And she gave Bubber a dime, too.

We bought a quart of milk and a box of sugar cookies and stood in an alleyway and ate everything.

When it got dark we went home. A woman passed, carrying a fish wrapped in newspaper. "Go home, children," she sang. "Your mother is waiting for you."

We didn't go directly into our building. What if the man in the plaid jacket was waiting for us in the hall? We went into the next building and climbed the stairs to the roof. The wind was whistling around the chimneys. Between the two buildings, there was a narrow space, a quick step across. I went first and put out my hand to Bubber.

He shook his head.

"I won't let you fall. Just don't look down."

So he looked down and then I looked down— six stories of brick wall to the cement alley below. I hopped back and forth a few times. "See. It's easy." I went back and forth again. "Come on."

He shook his head.

"You're not going to fall. I've done it a million times."

He kept shaking his head.

"All right, wait a minute." I found a piece of clothesline, tied one end to a pipe on my side and the other end on his side. I crossed back. "Hold the rope," I said. "Cross." I was so sick of waiting for him I grabbed his hand and yanked him over. He came flying across, and I went over backward with him on top of me. He started to cry. It was a dumb thing to do, but I'm just not patient enough.

"Come on," I said, "stop bawling. You did it."

Bubber sat up and looked around.

"You want to do it again?"

He shook his head. "N. O."

In the house, we took our shoes off and sat on the floor so we wouldn't scrape the chairs. We ate a can of beans in the dark, with just the light from the stove. I was worried about the people downstairs and Mrs. Chrissman next door. I wanted to go down to check the mail, but I was afraid she'd see me. I could go out the window again and over the roof. "I'm coming, too," Bubber said. He didn't want to stay in the house alone.

Two more times over the roof with him? "Forget it." I turned the radio on low and we got on our parents' bed.

15

The next day it was raining and we didn't go out. I didn't even go down to check the mail. When my father got my letter he'd call. I kept listening for the phone in the hall downstairs, but it didn't ring all day.

The next morning was Friday and it was still raining, and for no reason I felt good. Maybe because it was Friday. My father was going to finish work today and be here tomorrow. Maybe even tonight. Once he got my letter he'd jump on the first train and come straight home.

For breakfast, I made the last of the oatmeal, then we went downstairs to wait for the mail. I was a little jumpy going by Mrs. Chrissman's door. I could hear Murray and his mother yelling at each other.

"Wear your rubbers," Mrs. Chrissman said.

"It's not raining, Mom."

The mailbox was empty, but it was still early. I

saw the mailman going into section Z. Bubber and I waited in the hall. When Murray came bouncing down the stairs, we ducked under the stairs. Then Mrs. Engel, our downstairs neighbor, stood right in front of where we were hiding and looked into her mailbox. She opened her umbrella and went out.

When the mailman came, we were in another part of the hall. I heard him opening the boxes. One key he carried on a long chain opened all the boxes. I heard the mail drop into the slots, then the doors were banged shut.

I told Bubber to wait while I checked our mailbox.

"What are you doing, boy?" Mr. Brooks, the janitor, was standing by the stairs, smoking a cigarette. Narrow face the color of prune juice. Mr. Brooks was nobody to fool with. He was skinny, but all muscle, strong from all the barrels of ashes and garbage he lifted. He was strict, didn't allow any chalking on his buildings or ball playing in the courts. Once he'd chased Bubber right into the house for playing ball in the hall.

"You expecting a letter?" he said.

"Yes, sir," I said.

"Open the box, then. You got the key. Maybe Uncle Sammy is sending you a lot of money." He smiled, flashed gold.

I opened it. There was a letter.

"Where's your father? I haven't seen him for a while."

"Working."

"That's good. Where's your mother? Haven't seen her lately."

"She's sick."

"Oh, that's it. I seen you come home with the groceries. You taking care of your mother? That's a good boy. You won't have your mother forever."

I ran upstairs. The letter was from the hospital. I was afraid to open it till I was inside our apartment. It was from my mother, but it was somebody else's handwriting.

"My dear children, did you hear from Daddy? Is he home? Why hasn't he come to see me yet? I wrote him the first day I was here.

"I can't even write this letter, I'm so tired and weak. A kind lady is helping me. My precious children, don't worry. I'm going to be all right. If Daddy's not home today, I'm sure he'll be there tomorrow. Meanwhile, I want you to be good and don't aggravate Buba. She's not used to young children."

I read the letter over again. She didn't say anything about coming home. She didn't know Buba was sick and we were alone.

The bell rang, someone kicked the door. It was

Bubber. I let him in. He kicked at me, then ran and hid in the closet.

"What's the matter?"

"You left me downstairs. You forgot me."

"I just came up for a second." I put the letter in my back pocket. Bubber was hiding in Momma's bathrobe. "Okay," I said, "okay." I patted him on the back.

After a while he quieted down. "Did a letter come?" he said.

I showed him Momma's letter. "Daddy's coming. She wrote him." But if my mother wrote him the day she got sick, why wasn't he here already?

I went and looked out the window. Should we wait here for him? What if he didn't come today? Should we go back to my grandmother's? What if he was coming off the train right now? What if Grandma was still sick and didn't want us? Should I tell her Momma was sick, too, and in the hospital and we didn't have anyplace else to go? That might make her feel worse. And what if my father came and we weren't here? But he'd know we were at my grandmother's. I could leave him a note.

There was a knock on the door, a loud knock. Someone was really banging on the door. "I know you boys are in there. Open up!" It was the man in the plaid jacket again.

16

We went out the window and over the roof. It was still raining. We went back to the burned-out restaurant. I didn't know where else to go. I wanted to stay near our house in case my father came. Later, maybe, if we had to, we'd go to my grandmother's. I went down into the cellar on the dumbwaiter, then rode Bubber down. He didn't like the dark, but he liked the room I'd found.

He sat on the springs. "Are we going to sleep here?"

I looked at the stove. I looked at the little window. I looked at the dirty walls. I thought about my parents. Maybe a letter had come. Yeah, and maybe McKenzie's man was sitting right by the mailbox. Or was he on the stairs by our apartment? Or on the next landing, where he could watch and not be seen? Or did he have a skeleton key, and was he inside our house right now, waiting for us?

"This will be our cave," Bubber said. He held his hands over the stove like there was heat in it. "This is where we'll cook." He bounced on the springs. "And we'll sleep on this good bed." Then he got up and "poured" himself a cup of cocoa, sipped it, then blew on it. "It's too hot. You want a marshmallow in yours, Tolley?"

That's one thing about my brother, he has a terrific imagination. I get caught up in the worry of things. But not Bubber. He can be a baby sometimes, but he makes himself at home wherever he is.

Stay here? It was just a dirty storage room in a cellar. How were we going to stay here? What if we made a fire and somebody saw our smoke? What if they saw us going in and out? But then I shut up my dumb, practical mind. If Bubber said it was a cave, then let it be a cave. Our cave. A cave under the city.

We could stay here tonight, maybe even for a couple of nights, just till my father came home.

17

We slept together on the bare springs that night. Every time Bubber moved I woke up. I heard the trains going by and thought about my mother and my father. Was she better? Was my father closer? Was he home yet? What if he was home and we weren't there? He'd think we were with my grandmother, but I hadn't left him a note. McKenzie's man had come too fast.

In the morning, Bubber found a piece of a Tootsie Roll in his pocket, covered with lint. We sat on the springs, taking turns sucking it. Bubber made loud smacking sucks. "What are you doing?"

"Sucking a lollipop." He licked his lips.

"What flavor?"

"What flavor is yours, Tolley?"

"Lemon."

"Mine is lemon, too."

I yawned. He yawned. I crossed my legs, he

crossed his. Why was he copying me? I didn't want him doing everything I did. My mother was always telling me I had to be a good example to Bubber. I wasn't that good. I didn't want to be that good.

"If you could wish anything you wanted, Tolley, what would you wish first?"

"Momma to be out of the hospital."

"What would be your next wish, Tolley?"

"What's yours?"

"Bacon and eggs. I'm hungry."

"You think you're the only one?" I looked up the dumbwaiter shaft. "Come on, let's go."

I sent Bubber up first and then he helped me come up. It was just as hard as it had been the first day. "We need a ladder."

"Poppa's got lots of ladders."

My father kept his ladders chained in the carriage room. He wouldn't like it if I carried one of his ladders all the way over here.

From the outside, I looked for our window in the cellar room. It was just a small square hole in the wall. You couldn't even see the chimney hole. We explored through the weeds and the high grass. There were trails crisscrossing through the empty lots. I found a chair with three legs and carried it back. Behind a store by the restaurant we found an open faucet. Bubber put his mouth to it and drank. Then I drank. We played around with the water for a while, piled some rocks near it and made a little pool.

Bubber found wild grapes. The vines were crawling all over. Sour grapes and full of tiny seeds. I put a bunch of grapes in my mouth, ate them, seeds and all.

Bubber stuck out his tongue. "What color is my tongue, Tolley?"

"Green, with white polka dots."

"Stop it. Your mouth is purple."

"Let me see your tongue again."

He stuck it out.

"You need a doctor."

He spit a seed at me. I spit ten at him. Every time he spit one at me, I spit ten at him. I hate to admit it, but I was enjoying myself.

"Stop it," he said finally.

"You started it."

"Who's the baby now, Tolley?"

All day I thought about going back to our apartment. What if my father was there already? But what if McKenzie's man was waiting for us? It was safer in the lots, where we could disappear into the high grass or duck back into the cave.

An old Christmas tree with all the branches lopped off was leaning against an apple tree. I climbed it and shook down a bunch of yellow apples. Bubber watched me bite into one. "You just ate a worm, ugh."

"You want the other half?"

"Ugh. Ugh, ugh, ugh." Bubber filled his pockets.

Coming down the tree, I got my brilliant idea.

We carried the Christmas tree back and dropped it down the shaft. Then we climbed down. It made a perfect ladder.

Later it started to rain again, so we stayed inside the cave and ate the rest of the apples.

18

I woke up and lay there, looking up at the window square. Black square. Blackness all around me. How late was it? I listened and didn't hear anything. Was my father home? Was he looking for us? Was he sleeping in the house? It was too quiet. No traffic, no trolley cars, no trains. The newspapers we were sleeping on had slid off. I picked them up and covered Bubber. Then I went out.

There was nobody on the street. The air smelled wet like the ocean. Fog stuck to everything, the lights and the light poles and buildings. Far away I heard engines and foghorns.

A car passed, its lights poking at the fog. I stayed close to buildings. The only sound was the slap of my shoes. I saw the lights of an approaching car and hid till it passed. Then a cat scared me. I kicked at it. I thought it was going to jump on my back.

In our building I checked the mailbox. The light

wasn't good and I had to feel around in the box. There was a postcard. I put it in my pocket and went quietly up the stairs.

At our door, I slid the key carefully into the lock, the tumblers fell, the door clicked open. I remembered nights I was supposed to be home early and came in late, sliding in like a snake, praying my parents were asleep. Was my father sitting up in the living room, waiting for me now?

The apartment was empty. A little light came in from the street. The pipes rattled. I tiptoed through both rooms, opened all the closet doors, then shut them again. I even looked under the bed. Then I went into the bathroom and turned on the little light over the sink and read the postcard. It was from my father.

It was a picture postcard. The Capitol on one side. And on the other there was just room for a couple of lines. "Dear Family, Job ended in Baltimore. Looking for work in D.C. I miss my boys and my dear wife. Morris Holtz."

I turned the postcard over and over again. The picture on one side and three stingy lines on the other. Like every word cost him a dollar. "Looking for work in D.C. . . ." Where was his address? Where was he staying? Did he have my letter? And my mother's? Where was I going to write him now? How was I going to tell him what had happened?

I saw my scared face in the mirror. I hit my head against the wall, made my brains rattle. I had to think and I couldn't think. What was I going to do? Should we go to my grandmother's? Should we stay here? Should we stay where we were? I didn't want to go out again. I was home, it was warm here and our beds were here, and everything was nice.

I went from one room to the next, from one side of the apartment to the other. On the floor near the door, I saw a piece of paper and picked it up. Notices from the landlord were slipped under our door. I went to the window with it. The paper had an official-looking seal on the top. "Subject: Brothers, Tolman and Robert Holtz. . . ." I didn't read the rest of it. It was McKenzie again.

I spread out a blanket and started throwing in things we could use. Clothes, another blanket, candles, cans of food, a pot and a frying pan, and a kitchen knife. I found a box of wooden matches, sugar and salt, and a tin of Dutch cocoa. My father's tools were in the back of the closet. The toolbox was too heavy to carry, but I took a hammer and some nails and the saw he kept on the shelf, oiled and wrapped in newspapers.

Even Bubber's rabbit. Momma had made it for him when he was little. It used to be yellow and furry with two red-button eyes. Now it was mangy, only one eye left, and the insides coming out of the nose. Bubber still slept with it. I threw it in and tied the four corners of the blanket together.

The last thing I did was write a note.

"Dear Pop, Bubber and I are all right. We are not far away. We have a place to sleep and we are waiting for you to come home. Your son, Tolley."

I put the note in the corner of the picture that hung in the hall. It had an old-time country scene with cows and farm women in long dresses gathering grain. That was where my parents always left notes for each other.

Outside, I threw the bundle over one shoulder and walked that way for a while, and then threw it over the other shoulder. Something sharp dug into my side. *Tolley . . .* I heard my mother's voice. *What are you doing? You're going to live in a hole in the ground? Where's your common sense?*

Was this one of my stupid things? I stopped to get my breath. A dog came at me out of a dark alley. I heard the chain and his nails on the cement. I ran. Farther on, I leaned against a car. My eyes shut. *Tolley . . .*

Leave me alone, Momma. I just want to be someplace.

A man came out of the fog. I didn't move. I was so tired I didn't care. He could have murdered me and I wouldn't have moved. I was leaning against the car's fender and he walked right by me and didn't say a word.

When I came to the edge of the lot, I threw the bundle over. Then I slid over the side, fell straight down into the bushes, and lay there. I heard a milk wagon pass, heard the steady *clop clop clop* of the horse's hooves. The foggy sky was going soft and gray. A bird on a telephone pole sang. Sang and sang, the same thing, over and over again. *Tolley, what are you doing? ... Tolley, what are you doing? ... Tolley ...*

19

Bubber wasn't in the cellar room. "Bubber?" I couldn't see anything. I felt the bed. I felt under the newspapers. "Bubber." I could hardly say his name. I struck a match. Then another one. They kept going out. I felt around the cot again. I heard something, the sound of breathing, that dog's breath. Bubber was underneath the bed. He lay in the dirt staring at me.

I lit another match. "What are you doing?" There were cobwebs on his face. "I just went to get our stuff from the house."

He stared at me. "What do you want?" I said. "I'm here. What did you wake up for, anyway?"

"Is Momma home?"

I pulled him out. "Not yet."

"Is Poppa home?"

"No!"

His arms fell to his sides and he started to cry.

I hated him when he cried. He cried with his eyes shut and his mouth open with drool coming out of it. "What can I do about it? Wipe that drool off your face. Here's your stupid rabbit."

Bubber held the rabbit on his lap and he was talking to it silently, just moving his lips. He shook the rabbit's head and it talked back to him. I was sure they were talking about me. "What did you say?"

Bubber shook his head. "Rabbit says."

"What does rabbit say?"

"Tolley's too rough. Tolley tore my ear off."

"I did not. That rabbit was torn when I got it."

Bubber put his arm around the rabbit. "Rabbit doesn't like Tolley's loud voice. He says poor Bubber woke up and mean Tolley was gone."

"Okay, next time I'll wake both you and your rabbit up. Neither of you is that perfect, either. How about all the times I had to look for you?"

"What times?"

"What times! What have you got, a mind or a hole in your head? You're always wandering off. 'Where's Bubber? Tolley, go find Bubber.' I don't get mad at you and hide under the bed and not talk."

"You hit me."

"When?"

"All the time. You yank my arm. You push me."

"Not that hard."

86

"It hurts, you always hurt me."

"I don't do it on purpose."

"It hurts!"

"Forget it, will you! From now on, you be the big brother. I resign." I lay down, pulled a blanket over me. "Big brother Bubber, where are you? I'm hungry. I have to go doo-doo."

Bubber pushed me. "Stop it."

"That hurts. You hurt me. You always hurt me."

"Don't!" Bubber put his hand over my mouth.

"Big Brother Bubber." I popped my finger in my mouth. "I want some bread and butter. Butter, Bubber, for your baby brudder."

He pulled the finger out of my mouth. "No sucking, you dope."

"I'm hungry," I whined. "Feed me. Feed meee." I threw myself around. "Tolley's little tummy hurts."

"I don't say that, you liar." He whacked me.

"Owwww! Bubber hit me. Bubber hit me. Owwww! Feed me. You're supposed to take care of me."

He got the can of salmon. "Where's the can opener?"

"No can opener?" I'd forgotten the can opener. I threw the can against the wall. Then I got the hammer and a nail and punctured the top all the way around and pried the lid off. I didn't know how hungry I was till I smelled the fish.

20

A board on a couple of boxes made a combination shelf and bench. Bubber sat right down on it with his rabbit. Our clothes went into the boxes, the pot went on the stove, and the candles on the shelf. I hung my father's hammer and saw on the wall.

I was cleaning out the stove when I heard Bubber say, "Hello."

I swung around and there was a dog, his sniffy nose in the door. "Where'd you come from? How did that dog get in here?"

"King!" Bubber greeted him.

"Do you know him?"

"Here, King." The dog backed away. Bubber got the salmon can. "King is hungry. Here, King, here, good boy." The dog came back and got his nose right into the can, licked it clean. "Do we have some more, Tolley? King wants more salmon."

"We can't feed dogs." I nudged the dog. I didn't kick him or anything, just toed him, so he'd get the idea. "Leave. Good dog. Good-bye." The dog flattened himself. He was rust colored with long straggly hair. "Come on, get out of here," I said. "You're not getting any more food here."

"Stay there, King, don't go. Wait for Bubber."

The dog slunk around me and settled down at Bubber's feet.

"What I want to know is how you got down here," I said. "You sure didn't climb down the ladder, unless you're part monkey." The dog blinked his eyes. "This dog knows something." I lit a candle. "Come on, Tramp, show me how you got down here."

"Call him King," Bubber said. "He won't listen if you call him Tramp. Come on, King honey, show us how you got down here."

The dog was smart. He knew just what we wanted, and he ran back into the darkest part of the cellar. We followed him. Cold air blew across my legs and the candle blew out. King was gone.

Bubber pointed to a break in the foundation, a hole just big enough for a dog to get through. I got a board and knocked out some loose bricks and made the hole big enough so I could slide through. I came out under the back stairs.

Bubber crawled out after me. "It's a secret entrance." He had his arms around the dog. "King found it. Do you like him now?"

That morning, we found a lot of good stuff for the cave. We found bottles and filled them at the faucet. Then we found an abandoned car that still had its seats. We carried the backseat to the restaurant and dropped it down the dumbwaiter. That was going to be Bubber's new bed. "See," he said. "King brought us good luck."

Across the trolley tracks there were some houses and more empty lots. There was a garden in one of the lots. It had a fence around it made out of old doors. Through the cracks, we saw cabbages and pumpkins and an apple tree. One branch was hanging over our side.

Bubber jumped. I threw a stick up and some apples fell off. Good red apples. We started eating as fast as we could. Bubber took a bite, then gave King a bite, then took a bite for himself. I threw King my apple core and he ate that, too. I was knocking down more apples when an old man came running toward us, shouting and cursing.

We ran, crossed the trolley tracks back to our side, and didn't stop running until we were back behind the restaurant. We crouched there with King. One thing about that dog, he was smart enough not to bark.

It was warm there next to the foundation. Later, when it got dark and cold, we went inside. I started a fire in the stove with newspapers and wood we'd collected. I made cocoa with water and sugar. The room warmed up fast. It was sort of smoky, but when I checked outside, the smoke was hidden by the trees.

That night, Bubber and King slept on the car seat. Outside, I heard the wind blowing and branches rubbing against the building. When the train passed, it shook the building. King muttered in his sleep. Did dogs dream? I was trying to remember the last time my mother made supper for us. What did we eat? Boiled chicken, steamed onions and carrots, and mashed potatoes. I dreamed white bread and yellow butter. I dreamed. . . .

21

In the gray light I guessed it was six o'clock. I crept past Bubber and King. I was hungry. I was starved. I wanted food. I went to Allerton Avenue and down the steps to Lazinski's grocery store. The smell of fresh rolls dug a hole in my belly. Mr. Lazinski, in a clean white apron, was waiting on a customer. He cut the round of Muenster cheese with a long knife. The cheese was orange on the outside and pale yellow inside. "A little over, all right? Anything else, my lady?"

I was so hungry I wanted everything. The yellow Muenster cheese, the white farmer cheese, the rows of white eggs in the crate, the fat brown rolls, the sugared donuts.

The woman looked at me, looked me up and down and up again. What was she looking at? I didn't know her. I picked out a half dozen fresh rolls from the bin and waited my turn. It was all I could do not to tear off a piece of roll and eat it right there.

"Where have you been sleeping?" Mr. Lazinski said. "In a coal bin?"

I brushed my face. "I've been looking for deposit bottles. I guess I got a little dirty."

"A little dirty. I guess you did." Mr. Lazinski and the woman laughed. I put the rolls on the counter. "What else?" Mr. Lazinski said to me. I pointed to a box of Cream of Wheat high on the shelves and he nudged it down with a catcher on a long pole.

"Eggs."

"How many?"

"Six." I ordered bacon and sweet butter and a quart of milk. I watched him cut out a chunk of butter, then stick the knife back into the wooden tub.

"What else, my dirty prince?"

I added two jelly donuts. I had to bite my lip to stop myself from ordering more. "That's all. Charge it," I said.

Mr. Lazinski frowned. I watched his broad red hands as he studied the book. "You don't have anything to give me, Holtz?"

"My mother said she'd pay you soon."

"You don't have any money with you?"

I shook my head.

"I told you last time. I can't keep giving you credit."

"My mother—we're a little short . . ."

Mr. Lazinski had his arms around my order.

"She said definitely Friday."

"Today is Friday."

My hands were on the edge of the counter. Dirty fingernails, dirty fingers, dirty hands. I put my hands in my pockets. Empty pockets. I wished I had a dollar so I could put it on the counter. I prayed for a dollar. I looked at the food. Just one dollar.

"Well, you want me to hold it?"

I couldn't speak. I couldn't say yes. I couldn't say no. I grabbed the two doughnuts and ran out of the store.

I ate one doughnut and then I felt sick. I was still hungry, but it was worse than hunger. I was ashamed. Ashamed to be on the street. Ashamed to be seen. I saw people looking at me. Look at that boy. Look at the dirt on him. He's a thief.

I kept my eyes down and searched for money in the street, so I could go back and pay Mr. Lazinski. I wanted to find a quarter, a dime, even a nickel. I was always finding money. I was lucky that way. I had quick eyes. You needed quick eyes in the city. My eyes were everywhere. I always found money— once I'd found five dollars and given it to my mother. But now all I wanted was a dime.

Pop. In my head, I wrote my father another letter. *Dear Pop, where are you? Send me some money. We're all right. Bubber is hungry all the time and I am, too. If you don't come soon, maybe I should let him go to the orphan home and let somebody take care of him.*

Behind some stores I found a couple of deposit bottles. A man and a woman rummaged through the garbage. They were collecting bottles and rags in a baby carriage. They stopped when they saw me, saw the bottles in my hand. I got out of there fast, then handed in the bottles at a candy store on Burke Avenue. There was a telephone booth in back. I shut the door and dropped in the nickel. The phone rang in our section. It was on the wall on the second floor. Next to it there was a row of buttons for each apartment. I imagined the door of our apartment opening on the fourth floor and my mother running down . . . or my father.

"Hello?" A man answered the phone. "Who do you wish to speak to?"

My tongue was stuck in my throat.

"Hello? What apartment, please?"

"Holtz," I said.

"One minute."

I heard the phone drop and hit the wall. Now he must be pushing the buzzer. It was ringing in our apartment. He wouldn't go up and knock on our door. He'd wait till he heard our door open.

He'd call up, "Holtz—telephone," and then he'd go back to his apartment. I listened, strained as hard as I could. Did I hear steps? Was Momma coming down the stairs?

"Hello." The man came on the phone again. "Nobody answers. Nobody's home."

"Try once more," I said. "Push it harder. Maybe they didn't hear."

"I pushed it enough. They don't answer. Goodbye." And he hung up.

I went outside. I walked right into traffic.

Dear Pop, Do you see what I'm doing? Are you listening? Sometimes I don't care what happens to me. You'd better come home. Bubber has a dog now and we're living in a pretty good place. Momma's waiting for you to come back. We are, too. Your son, Tolley.

In our lot I pushed through the bushes, then slid through the hole into the cellar. I smelled damp earth and burned wood and the dog smell.

King came out to investigate, then Bubber. "Tolley. What did you bring us?"

I took the doughnut out of my pocket. I gave it to Bubber and licked the jelly from my fingers.

22

"What day is it?" I asked Bubber.

"I don't know."

"Saturday. Don't you know anything?" I had told Mr. Lazinski my mother would pay him on Friday. "It *is* Friday," Mr. Lazinski had said, making me feel like a dirty liar and a beggar.

"When are we going out?" Bubber said.

"Never." I looked at him the way Mr. Lazinski had looked at me. I sat on a box and fed the fire. I didn't care what day it was. I wasn't going back to that store. I wasn't going out. I wasn't doing anything.

"I'm hungry."

"Don't bother me." We were going to pay Lazinski. Sometimes people were short. It didn't mean they weren't going to pay. We weren't deadbeats. I saw Mr. Lazinski's fat round face and his fat arms holding on to his groceries.

Bubber went out. I heard him calling King.

I lay there. My mind went to my mother and my father. Was there a letter? Had my father written? Was there news from the hospital? Something flashed in my stomach and in my brain. I saw the row of mailboxes, gleaming like the sun, and then there was nothing. Then I didn't think anymore. I was hungry.

I dug my fists into my stomach. Then I drank water, a lot of water.

I slept. Bubber was in and out. I woke up and heard him calling King again. I heard him singing, one of those crazy songs of his. "Jack and Joe went up the pole to catch a kitty cat. Jack fell down and Joe fell down and kitty cat laughed."

The next time I woke up, he was there with an apple. "Where'd you get this?"

"You still sleeping?" His breath was hot and he smelled like rotten apples.

I pushed him away. I didn't want to eat the apple. If I ate it, I'd start thinking about food again. But then I took a bite.

Bubber leaned on me. "Don't stand on top of me."

He lay down on the car seat and covered himself up. Later he woke. "Make the fire," he said. His teeth started to click.

"Cut it out." I thought he was faking. He sniffled

and picked his nose. "Will you blow your nose."

He sucked snot. "I don't have a handkerchief."

"Use newspaper."

"Newspaper hurts."

His head was hot. His breath smelled. "You're sick." Why did he have to get sick? I sat there listening to him sniffling. That green snot going in and out of his nose. It was making me sick, too.

What did my mother do when I was sick? She felt my head, she made me stick out my tongue. The doctor came and listened to my chest with the stethoscope he took from his little black satchel. He made me put out my tongue and stuck a wooden stick all the way back down my throat till I gagged. After that, he wrote a prescription on a little pad and told my mother to keep me in bed and give me lots of liquids.

I made the fire and covered Bubber with my blanket. I gave him water. He tossed around. He was talking in his sleep. "King ran away. He was hungry. Let's go look for him . . . look for him, Tolley."

"Tomorrow. When you feel better."

His eyelids fluttered. Then he sat up and said, "The butcher's giving him a bone. Give him the bone!"

That night he had a fever again. I felt his forehead. I told him I wanted him to be better in the morning. He said he would be. By the light of the fire, I could see his big dark eyes and his soft baby mouth.

The next day all he wanted to do was drink. The sniffles were gone. He kept throwing off the blankets and complaining about the heat, then a minute later he'd tell me he was cold.

"I'm going out," I said. "I'm going to get you some medicine."

In the window of the drugstore on Burke Avenue, there was a pharmacist's balance scale and a mortar and pestle. Over the door it said Ex-Lax in blue letters. A doorbell jingled as I entered. The druggist came around to the back of the counter, wiping the corner of his mouth. "Yes, young man, what can I do for you?"

I smelled salami. It smelled so good it made me dizzy. "What's good for a cold?"

"Do you have a prescription?"

"It's for my brother."

"Best thing is to stay in bed." He showed me cough medicine and throat lozenges and nosedrops. "Vicks is good for the chest, just rub it right in."

"Could I do some work for you? I'm strong."

The druggist sighed. "No money?"

"I can sweep, or wash the window."

"Sorry, I can't afford to hire anyone. The best thing for your brother is rest and lots of liquids.

Orange juice, chicken broth, tea. He can have toast, too."

I went to the door. *Orange juice, chicken broth, tea, and toast. Orange juice, chicken broth, tea, and toast.*

"Young man." The druggist called me back. "Here." He handed me aspirin powder in a white paper. "Have your mother give this to your brother mixed with a little juice or milk." I took the aspirin. "Well, go on," he said. "That's all."

Outside, a milk wagon stood at the curb, dripping water from the block of ice inside. The horse had the feed bag on. He looked at me. What do you want? The milkman took a rack of bottles and ran into a building. In the back of the wagon were cases and cases of milk in long-necked bottles. I reached in and took one. The horse stamped his feet.

Back in the cellar, I fed Bubber the cream off the top of the milk. Then I gave him the aspirin and more milk. He took long gulps.

I drank, then lay down. I'd stolen a bottle of milk. Was it wrong? It was stealing, but was it wrong? I did it for Bubber. And me, too. We were hungry. I didn't feel guilty. When I took the jelly doughnuts, I was ashamed. Not now. When you're hungry enough and sick, too, you can take things. Was that true?

"I took it," I said.

"What?" Bubber's lips looked thick and swollen.

"I didn't pay for the milk. I swiped it."

"What?"

"I took it," I said. "Swiped it. I stole it. You drank it. You think it's wrong? Okay. Next time, I'll drink it all myself."

23

The next morning Bubber slept and I went out again. On every block I saw people eating, on the street and at lunch counters. The horse had on his feed bag. The birds ate the oats he spilled. At a hot-dog cart, a woman bought a hot dog thick with relish.

I sniffed and swallowed. On every block there were smells. The cheese smell from the grocery store, the bread smell from the bakery, the chicken smell in the poultry store, and the smell of malteds from the candy store. People were going in and out of stores, buying and chewing, carrying out bags of groceries. "Carry your bag, lady?"

The woman wore a dark cape and a big floppy hat. She looked rich.

"For a dime," I said.

She shifted her bag to her other arm. She had little fat pillows over her eyes, and where her eyebrows used to be there was just a pencil stripe. She walked away from me.

I caught a glimpse of myself in the store window. There were leaves stuck in my hair and dirt on my face. I spit on my finger and cleaned my chin.

A man pushed a wagon full of bananas up a hill. I pushed with him. On top of the hill he gave me a banana. I ate it. A truckload of crated chickens was being unloaded. "Want some help?" The driver shook his head.

A group of black women stood in the sun by the bank. A skinny woman in a brown coat caught my eye and smiled. There was a wide space between her front teeth. "Your mother send you to get some help for the house, sonny?"

"My mother's sick."

"Yeah." The woman's eyes slid away. "Everybody's got troubles."

In front of Woolworth's, a man with no legs sat on a wheeled platform. He had pencils in a cup and another cup for coins.

I stood by the stairs to the el. How did you beg? I didn't have a hat or a cup. I waited, looking for the right person, the right face. People went by me. I let ten people go by and then ten more. Every face was squeezed tight. A woman smiled. I thought she was smiling at me. I kept my eyes down and put out my hand. She put a penny in my hand.

At a fruit stand, the oranges were like a hill of gold balls. There were so many of them. All I wanted was one. A small woman in a black cardigan was spitting on the apples and polishing them on her sleeve. Underneath the bins was a box of rotten fruit and vegetables.

"Want me to take that away?"

"What did you say?" She put her hands into her sweater pockets.

"That." I pointed to the box.

"You want that rotten fruit?"

"I'll take it away for you."

"What are you going to do with it?"

"Feed it to my dog."

"Your dog eats bananas? Take it." She handed me a bag. "But leave me the box."

I filled the bag. There was a lot of good stuff. "I'll sweep the store for you. Free."

"Be my guest."

I swept the store and the sidewalk. Then I carried boxes of lettuce and celery from the back of the store. "What else? You got anything else for me to do?"

"Don't you go to school?"

"I stayed home today because my mother's sick."

She paid me a quarter and threw some good potatoes and carrots into the bag. "For your dog," she said.

On the way back, I passed a butcher shop and asked for a bone for my dog and the butcher gave it to me. Then I went into a bakery and bought an old bread for a penny.

Bubber was excited when I showed him what I had. I cut the bad part out of an orange and gave him the good part. "Tolley, did you swipe it?"

"I don't steal."

"The milk—"

"Just shut up about that."

Bubber wanted to give the bone to King. "Just wait," I said. I made a fire. Then I made soup the way I'd seen my mother do it. I put everything in the pot, the bone and the potatoes and carrots, and let it cook.

The smell made us crazy. We ate out of the pot with our fingers, then soaked up the liquid with the dry bread. King came back, and he lay in the corner cracking the bone.

That was one day. The next day we were hungry again. Things didn't go the way they had the day before. The only thing that was the same was that we were hungry.

We were hungry every day. And every day we looked for food. If I got hungry enough, I grabbed a bottle of milk.

One day we went to the zoo and watched the

animals being fed. The seals got a bucket of fish. The lions got big chunks of red meat, and the elephants were eating loaves of pumpernickel bread. Bubber said he was going to slip between the bars and get a bread. I dragged him away. In the monkey house, though, I spotted a banana next to the bars in the cage. The chimp was up on a shelf. I reached in and got the banana. The chimp watched, then pointed a finger at me and started screaming.

We stayed in the zoo all day. In the shallows by the river we collected crayfish in a can. There were Cracker Jack boxes in every garbage can with Cracker Jacks stuck to the bottom. We found half-eaten sandwiches and ate those, too.

When it started to get dark, we drifted over to the train station. Not the one in our neighborhood. We went up the stairs and stood by the change booth. I got my nerve up and asked a man, "You got a nickel for the subway, mister?" I did it four or five times before I got a nickel. The man in the change booth was looking at us, so we went downstairs, but I couldn't get started again. I let Bubber do it. He never said anything, just stood there, smiling up at people with his hand out.

One day we got on the train and went to see my grandmother. Her door was locked. I pushed the buzzer a long time. Was she asleep? Still sick? In

107

the lobby Bubber went from chair to chair. I went back to my grandmother's door and pushed the buzzer and listened, then knocked.

A man came out from the apartment across the way. "She's in the hospital. Who're you?"

"Her grandson."

"She's in the hospital. Didn't anybody tell you?"

I went back and got Bubber. "Come on," I said, "Grandma's sleeping." And we went back to the cave.

24

Candles were for emergencies. Most nights the only light we had was from the fire. It was always out when we woke up, and one morning there was a thin sheet of ice in the water bottle. Every day it got colder, and we spent a lot of time gathering wood.

I hardly ever thought about the way we used to live. I hardly thought about my parents. If I did think about them, it was like something that had happened a long time ago. Like a story or a movie.

We were always together, Bubber and King and me. We went everywhere, but never to our old neighborhood. Bubber got food a lot of times when I couldn't, and King sniffed out good garbage.

I saved everything. Tin cans, bottles, and newspapers. I found some pieces of carpet in the garbage and put them on the floor, on our beds, and nailed one piece over the window.

One day it was so cold we couldn't stay in the cave. We went from building to building, warming our hands over the radiators. When anyone came, we went right out. "Where are we going?" Bubber said.

"We're walking."

"Where are we walking?"

"We're walking where we're walking." But then I thought, he's only in first grade, and I gave him a geography lesson. This way, traveling around the city, he would learn a lot. "The Bronx," I said, "is surrounded on three sides by water. On the east there's Long Island Sound and on the west there's the Hudson River. And on the south it's either the Harlem River or the East River, I don't remember which. So you could say that whatever way we're walking, we're walking toward the water. Unless we're going north. Now you tell me."

"The Bronx," he said, "is surrounded on three sides by water. On the east there's Long Island Sound and on the west there's the Hudson River. . . ."

"Very good," I said. "A plus and a gold star."

Bubber liked that. He wanted more. "Read that sign," I said, pointing to a drugstore. It said "Biologicals" and "Alka Seltzer." Bubber got the b sound and then he got stuck.

"Scratch that," I said, and I gave him something he knew. "What's two times one?"

"Two times one is two. Two times two is four. Two times three is six."

He knew a lot of his times tables for a first grader.

"Two times nine is eighteen. Two times ten is twenty."

"Okay. Good. Which way isn't the water? North, east, south, or west?"

"North."

"Good." Teaching Bubber helped make the time pass.

One night I went back to our building. Our windows were dark. I ran in and checked our mailbox, then ran out again.

Every day was different, and every morning Bubber said the same thing. "I'm hungry."

Sometimes we went to the library. They had good bathrooms. I read stories to Bubber and tried to get him to read some of the words. There were a lot of men in the library, reading the newspapers or sleeping with their heads on their arms.

One day we were walking along the edge of the tracks and saw something glinting through the bare trees. It was an abandoned 1929 Ford. The windows had been smashed and everything had been taken out, but in the bushes we found two wheels with the tires still on them. We rolled the tires to the junk man under the Third Avenue el. "We'll probably get five dollars for them," I told Bubber.

"We'll be rich," Bubber said. "What will we buy?"

"Nothing," I said. "We're going to save the money."

Bubber threw down the wheel. "Then you roll it. I'm not going."

"What do you want? I was just teasing. You want me to buy gloves?"

He nodded.

"How about me?"

"Two pairs of gloves," he said.

"Okay, what else?"

"Two Baby Ruths, two Mary Janes, two Milky Ways and—"

"Hold it, hold it. How about shoes?"

"Two pairs of shoes, two hats, two jackets, and two Mounds bars and two packs of candy cigarettes."

"Hold it, hold it, hold it. There's nothing left. We spent it all."

"Okay," Bubber said, "two pairs of gloves, then we go to the candy store."

"Okay. Start pushing."

The junkyard was in an old horse barn. There were auto parts piled on the floor—batteries and tires and carburetors—and hubcaps on the walls. The junk man came out to look at the wheels. He was fat and he wore khaki pants and a Sam Browne belt with a big ring of keys. "What'd they come off of?"

"A 1929 Ford."

"You got the other wheels? Bring the other wheels and I'll give you a good price."

"How much for these?"

He turned the wheels over. "I got a warehouse full of Ford wheels."

"It's a good tire. They're both good." I thought he'd give two dollars.

He kicked the tires. "Two bits. Two bits apiece. Quarter for each one." He pulled a greasy leather purse from his pocket.

"Is that all?"

He snapped his purse shut. "Forget it. Take your wheels out of here. I don't want them."

"What are we going to do with them?"

"That's your problem. I was only doing you a favor."

"Come on, Starkey, give the kid a break."

I looked around. The voice had come from the rag pile. A tall boy sat up and grinned at me. He wore a hat with the brim cut off and the crown cut out in diamonds and squares. He wasn't that much older than me. "Those wheels are worth two bucks apiece, at least."

"Hey, Whitey, what am I running, a charity or a

business?" He bit off the end of his cigar and spit it out. "Okay, kid, one buck. Take it or leave it."

Whitey nodded to me. "Take it."

I held out my hand. The junk man gave me a dollar.

25

When we left the junkyard, Whitey walked along with us. "Where are you kids going?" He took his cap off. He had a ring of red around his forehead, but his hair was white. "Bubber and Tolley, who gave you those funny names? And King, that's your dog? Some king. I had a dog once, a Doberman. Dobie. That's when we lived in the country. We always had a dog. Each of us kids had something. I had Dobie, my one sister had goats, and my other sister had a garden." He said *gah-dun*.

"Where's your dog now?" Bubber said.

"Same place my house is."

"Where's your house?"

"Where it's always been."

Bubber looked up at him. "Far away?"

Whitey nodded his head slowly. "Hy-annis."

"What's that?"

"In the ocean."

Bubber looked over to me. "Is he teasing?"

"He lives near the ocean. Cape Cod, it's like Orchard Beach, only it's far away. Don't ask so many questions."

"Did you run away from your house?" Bubber said.

"Did you?"

Bubber nudged me. "What should I say?"

"Shut your mouth!"

Whitey stopped at a candy store. "I need some smokes. You guys want something?"

I shook my head, but Bubber said, "I do!"

When Whitey went into the store, I walked Bubber away. "You ask too many questions. And we don't take things from people."

"Yes, we do," Bubber said. "You do."

"This is different. He's like us."

I could see Bubber thinking about it. "You mean his momma's sick, too?"

"Something like that." I wanted Whitey to like us. Maybe the three of us could stick together.

"Hey, Toll, Bub, wait up." Whitey had three cigarettes. He lit one and put the others behind his ears. He held the lit cigarette in the corner of his mouth, one eye screwed up. "Want a drag?"

I took it, rolled the cigarette between my fingers. Bubber watched. "You're not supposed to smoke."

"No kidding." I set the cigarette in the side of

116

my mouth the way Whitey had, puffed on it a couple of times, then handed it back.

Whitey handed Bubber a Hershey bar. "This what you want?"

Bubber looked at me. "Take it," I said. "You asked for it." Bubber shared it out, not forgetting King.

"Where do you kids live?" Whitey said. "Around here? You got a place for me to stay tonight?"

"You can sleep on my bed," Bubber said.

"That's my pal."

We stopped to buy bread, cheese, and milk. "You have any scraps for my dog?" Bubber asked the man. Ever since Bubber was sick, he'd changed. He'd gotten thin and sort of long, and he talked more to people.

When we got back to the cave, Whitey couldn't believe we went in through the hole. Bubber went through first. "You kids are like a couple of rats," Whitey said.

"It's easy." I showed him how I slid through on my back and he followed me.

In the cave, he looked around. "Nice. Nice. Gee, this is all right, Tolman. How'd you find this place? You are smart. The second I saw you, I knew you were going to be my friend. You and Bub."

I couldn't help smiling. I lit a couple of extra candles to make the place brighter and started the fire. It would be easy to fit another cot in here. After Bubber went to sleep, Whitey and I could talk and make plans.

We sat around the fire and ate. "I like to keep moving," Whitey said.

"Yeah." I folded a piece of bread around a slice of bologna. "It would be great to travel."

"One of these days, you're going to see me behind the wheel of a car. A Chevy or a Pontiac."

"If I had a car, I'd go see the mountains."

"I'm an ocean man, myself," Whitey said. "I don't like to get too far from the water."

"We've got the ocean here."

"Not much. I'm talking about the Atlantic Ocean, not Long Island Sound." He took a bite of his sandwich. "Where's your father and your mother?" He said it in that funny way of his—*fath-uh* and *moth-uh*. I shrugged. He took a cigarette from behind his ear and lit up. "It's getting nice and warm in here."

Bubber yawned and stretched out next to me.

"I like the heat," Whitey said. "I'm heading south. If I was south right now, I wouldn't need this coat, I wouldn't need these shoes. Walk on the beach with my pants rolled up. Hungry? Simple. Drop a line in the water and catch a fish. Tired? Sleep on the beach."

He closed his eyes. "They've got oranges down

there like horse balls up here. Pick oranges up off the street and eat them. They just rot otherwise. Cars roll right over them." He yawned. "Time for a little shut-eye."

I offered him the cot. "I'll sleep with Bubber."

"No, I'll sleep on the floor. I'm used to it." He wrapped his coat around himself and lay down by the door. "Are you going to keep the fire going?"

I went out and got some more wood. In Florida, we wouldn't need fires, not to keep warm. We could run around barefoot. It would be like going to the beach every day. We'd live on the beach. Everything would be there for the taking. All the food we wanted, on the ground and hanging from the trees.

I fixed the stove, "You really going to Florida, Whitey? When are you going?"

"I'm working on a ride. Starkey wants me to go down with him, maybe tomorrow, maybe in a couple of days. We'll take down a truckload of parts, then bring back a load of grapefruit and oranges."

"Would there be room for us?"

"What?" Whitey was falling asleep. "Sure, I'll ask Starkey. We can all help with the load."

I pulled the blanket over me. If Starkey said no, we could hide in back of the truck. Why did we have to go with Starkey, anyway? The three of us could go alone. We could hitch rides. Just stand Bubber by the side of the road, and we'd get all

119

the rides we wanted. Maybe we'd stop in Washington on the way and look around for my father.

Tolley. I heard my mother. *Tolley* . . . Her voice was weak and distant. Was this another of my crackpot ideas? How could we go to Florida? What about my parents? And my grandmother?

I tossed around, couldn't sleep. Florida . . . Whitey . . . the three of us. Three was better than two. Three heads were better than two. Three pairs of hands. We could work. Maybe we'd get a room. Bubber could even go to school. I'd write home—that would be the way to do it. Write and tell them we were in Florida and everything was easy.

26

In the morning Whitey wanted to know where the bathroom was. I slipped out through the hole. "Pick any bush you want."

He laughed. "You guys—" he said, and shook his head. "Come on. I'll show you something."

We went into a cafeteria on White Plains Road. We each took a ticket and followed Whitey to the men's room. He took off his coat and sweater. He had on a collarless shirt with cuff links. There was a rip in the seat of his pants. He washed his hands and his face, and combed his hair back till it lay flat and slick on his head. He brushed his teeth with his finger. Then he put his sweater and coat on again.

When he got done, Bubber and I washed. I looked in the mirror and scrubbed at a line of dirt clean around my neck. Whitey lent us his comb. I wet my hair and flattened it the way he did. Bubber's hair was a curly tangle that couldn't be combed.

At the counter, Whitey ordered coffee and a danish. "What do you guys want?"

Bubber ordered the same as Whitey. I felt in my pocket. A nickel was all I had left from yesterday, so I just ordered coffee.

"It's on me," Whitey said.

"I'm not that hungry in the morning." I didn't want him to think I was a moocher. We sat down. I put lots of sugar in my coffee and nibbled the raisins that Bubber picked out of his pastry.

Whitey ate fast, then said, "Come on," motioning to us to bring our cups and follow him. "I'll show you something else."

We went to the steam table, where you could draw free hot water, and we filled up our cups. Back at our table, we added the free sugar and milk. It tasted watery, but it was sweet and hot. Whitey switched our empty cream pitcher with another table and filled Bubber's cup. Then he sat back and lit his last cigarette. I sat back and looked around the way he did. Around us, people were eating, reading their papers. Nobody paid attention to us. It was nice sitting there, good to have someone else sitting with us. The cafeteria was warm, and it smelled good. The hot water in my belly made me feel full.

"What are we going to do?" I said. We. That sounded good to me.

"Gotta have some money. Gotta have some money." Whitey was singing, tapping on the table. Then he looked up, snapped his fingers, and winked at me. "Okay, got it. You guys wait right here. I won't be long." He left the cafeteria.

We sat there, waiting for him. "Where'd Whitey go?" Bubber said.

"Probably to talk to Starkey. We're going to go to Florida."

"King, too?"

"I don't know." I hadn't thought about that.

"I can't go without King."

"Do you know how far Florida is? Do you know what we're going to do down there? We're going to live on the beach. You're going to swim every day, and we're going to eat more and live better, and not have to wear all these clothes. You're not going to need shoes down there."

Bubber was listening with his mouth open. "We're going to sleep on the beach," I said. "Maybe we'll get a tent. Or maybe we'll rent a room. A real room, right by the ocean, with beds, and a toilet and running water. Whitey and I are going to get jobs and you're going to school."

Bubber shook his head.

"No? You want to work, too?"

"I don't want to go to school in Florida."

"What do you think, it's going to be a vacation forever? Well, that's okay, it doesn't matter that much. Maybe you don't have to go to school. You're going to learn a lot just being around Whitey and me."

We waited a long time. A girl and a boy came in with their father. They stood at the counter, waiting for their orders. The girl looked around at me a couple of times. I winked at her. I surprised myself. I think she noticed. I'd never winked at a girl before. Maybe I did it because of the way I was sitting, sprawled back like I was Whitey. I only wished I had a cigarette in my hand.

Bubber and I went back and filled up with hot water again. I swaggered a little bit when I went by the girl. The man behind the counter was watching us. I nudged Bubber and we drank up fast and went out.

For a while we stood in the entrance of the cafeteria. The girl came out with her father and brother. I was leaning against the building, my collar up and my hands in my pockets. I felt like Errol Flynn in *Captain Blood*. I looked after them till they disappeared behind the corner.

"I have to go," Bubber said.

"Then go." A car went by, and I thought I saw

Whitey. He'd do something interesting and different like that, come back for us in a car. *Jump in, Tolman! Come on, Bub. We're on our way to the sunny climes.*

Bubber butted me. "Tolley."

"Can't you hold it?" I didn't want to miss Whitey.

"I'm going to do it in my pants."

"Go in the cafeteria." I finally had to go back in with him. "Hurry up," I said. I was afraid Whitey would come while we were inside. If he was with somebody else, he wouldn't wait.

Outside, I looked up and down the street. Bubber was counting. "Seven . . . eight . . . ten . . . thirteen . . . "

"What are you counting?"

"People going in."

"How many?" I didn't care. It was just something to say. But I started counting, too. A fat man went in. "How many now?" I said to Bubber.

"Twenty."

"Wrong. Twenty and a half." He didn't get it. "The fat man," I said. "Twenty and a half."

"You can't have a half of a person, Tolley!"

It was a dumb conversation. That was the trouble with hanging around with a six-year-old kid all the time. Not that Bubber was dumb, but if Whitey were here, I wouldn't be playing counting games.

"Twenty-one," Bubber said.

"Twenty-two," I said.

We got up to forty, people were going in for lunch, and still no Whitey.

"When's Whitey coming?" Bubber said.

"That makes fourteen," I said.

"Fourteen what?"

"Fourteen times you asked the same dumb question."

"When's Whitey coming?"

"Fifteen."

"When's Whitey coming?"

"You'll know he's arrived when you see him coming."

We waited and we waited. We waited too long. Four o'clock, we were still waiting. I checked the round clock in the window of the shoe store.

"When's Whitey coming?"

I went to the corner and came back. I walked past the shoe store. I told myself not to check the time, but then I looked. He could still be coming. He could be coming right now.

The bells on the church chimed five times. I was standing on the corner near the fire alarm box. He wasn't coming. He'd ditched us. Suddenly I wanted to take the hammer and break the glass and sound the fire alarm. I had to walk away.

Later, we stood outside our house and looked

up at the unlit windows. Then I ran in to check the mailbox. It was empty.

That night I dreamed that my father had come back and he was sitting on the cot next to me. He was wearing a long coat like Whitey's and his shoes were covered with paint. I reached out for him. My hand touched cold iron. Next to me, I heard Bubber breathing.

27

It rained steadily for days. Upstairs, water dripped through the holes in the roof and ran down the insides of the walls. Even with the fire going we couldn't dry out the room. It was getting colder and we were sleeping together head to foot on the cot. Some nights I'd wake up with his feet in my face. I'd lie there and listen to his sniffling and the water popping and dripping down the walls.

Where was my father? I was thinking about him again, watching for him every day. I saw him hitchhiking, getting a ride on a truck or in a car, coming closer, coming home.

I didn't feel good a lot of times. My bones ached, and some days I didn't want to get out of bed. Bubber pulled at me. "I'm hungry. You want me to go without you?" I didn't care. Bubber and King went out alone. I had an idea they were begging.

Bubber brought me back a roll, a cupcake, a candy bar.

Other days we went out together. On rainy days, people wanted packages carried home. We worked together. Bubber carried packages as big as mine. When we had money, we went to a cafeteria and ordered soup and crackers, then sat there as long as we could. It was hard to stay awake. I'd lean on my elbow and Bubber would put his head down on the table. "I'm not sleeping," he said. "I'm talking to the table." If anyone said anything to us, we went someplace else. We weren't the only ones sitting with empty cups in front of us.

We were wet all the time. Bubber sniffled. On the train, he'd found a leather aviator's hat with earflaps. He wore it all the time. He needed a heavy jacket, so did I. We wore sweaters, one on top of the other. The worst thing was the holes in the soles of my shoes. I put cardboard in the bottom, but when it rained my feet got wet.

It rained and rained. The water sat in the cellar. One day it rained so hard, we couldn't stay inside and we couldn't stay out on the street. We stood in hallways for a while, then we went up to the el and asked the man in the coin booth if we could sit in the men's room and wait for our mother. There was a coal stove so it was warm, and we used the toilet.

All day we rode around on the trains. I liked being on the train. We were going someplace, even though we were only going in circles. We rode from the Bronx to Manhattan, over to Brooklyn and Coney Island, then back again. Once you got on the train, you never had to get off. You could go all over the city. If you got hungry, you could stop in a station and buy chocolate from the machine for a penny.

One day, on the way back from Coney Island, we stopped off in Manhattan at the Battery. I wanted Bubber to see the Statue of Liberty, but when we tried to sneak on the Staten Island ferry, we were chased. We ducked back on the train and rode up to the Museum of Natural History. Outside, by the chunk of meteorite that looked like black Swiss cheese, Bubber went around asking people for a nickel so he could call his mother. Then we bought hot dogs and orange soda from a street vendor. In the museum we mainly looked at the Indian exhibits—the Indian long boat and the hut cutaway showing an Indian family around a fire. Then we went to look at the dinosaur bones and the Great Blue Whale that filled up a room as big as the auditorium in school. Bubber fell asleep on the bench in the dinosaur room.

It was late and still raining when we got back to the cellar. King was outside. "Why's he out here?" Bubber said. "Go inside, boy!" When Bubber started to go in, King grabbed his leg. "He doesn't want me to go in."

Whitey's back, I thought. Then I thought the cops had discovered the cave. I went up on the street level and slipped inside. It was dark, but I could see something had happened. The roof was sagging down like a giant funnel and water was spilling through it into a hole where the floor had been. Underneath, where the cave was, the floor had fallen into the cellar and buried everything.

28

That night the three of us stayed under the stairs in back of the restaurant. In the morning we were out early. For a time we sat in back of a big Camel billboard to get out of the wind. The rain had stopped, but it was cold and the wind howled across the empty lots. It made the telephone poles shake and the grass whistle.

On top of a long empty hill we passed some houses and stores. Bubber stood on a corner with his hand out. I went into a bakery and asked for day-old bread. Begging.

The baker, flour over his face like a clown, said, "Three cents a loaf. Two loaves for a nickel."

I pulled out my pockets. I tried to look cute like Bubber.

The baker wiped his hands on his white apron. "What do you kids want from me? Nothing for nothing, my mother always said." Then he went in back. I thought he was going to call the police. I didn't care. I was too tired to run. What were we running for anyway? I couldn't remember anymore. The baker came back with two stale sandwich breads.

Bubber had a nickel. We bought a bottle of milk and went in back of the bakery and sat inside a big cardboard box. The breads were hard as rock. We soaked them in milk and ate them. We stayed there, out of the wind. Sometimes we slept. King went off and came back. When the baker went home, he threw a bag in the garbage, then banged down the lid. Bubber went out to investigate and came back with a handful of broken half-moon cookies. We gnawed them like bones and slept in the box that night like three dogs.

In the morning, we went on. We walked and we walked and we walked. I always thought you could blindfold me and turn me around ten times and I'd still be able to point straight to where I lived. But now I didn't know where we lived. We didn't live anywhere.

"Which way?" Bubber said. Any way. Maybe we were going in circles. It didn't matter. We didn't have anyplace to go. We didn't live anywhere anymore. When we lived in the cellar, I was ashamed. I didn't want anyone to know. We called it a cave, but it was just a cellar. Wet, dark, and dirty. Now it seemed like this wonderful place.

Near a movie house, King found a half-eaten hot dog in the street. I took a grab for it, but he swallowed it in one bite. I kicked him, and Bubber turned around and kicked me.

"Then go to hell," I yelled. "You and your dog both. Let him feed you." Then I walked away, without looking back.

I crossed railroad tracks. Ahead I saw the river and near it a bunch of shacks and junk houses banged together out of scraps of wood and rusted metal. People lived there. Some shacks had doors and windows, some had burlap or cardboard over the openings. One shack was half covered with a metal sign advertising Prince Albert tobacco. There were some kids playing in a woodpile. A dog barked at me.

I crossed more tracks and climbed down to the river. I sat on a rock, looking across the Hudson River to the Palisades on the Jersey side. The water made little sucking noises as it rose and fell on the rocks. A long way off, I heard a train whistle, then the distant pumping of the locomotive. I felt it coming in the ground. Moments later a train passed, the engine spitting sparks, white smoke flying from the wheels.

The long shriek of the train whistle reached down and twisted in me. I thought of my mother, my grandmother, and my father far away. And where was my brother? Bubber! I started back. A man stood by one of the shacks. "Did you see a little kid with curly hair?" I said.

A woman came out with an empty pail. "What's he want?" she said.

"How should I know?" the man said.

"Bubber!" I ran. I tripped over the railroad tracks. "Bubber!" I called. Why did I lose my temper? I wanted to kill myself for being so stupid. Why didn't I think? How could I lose him? *You lost your brother! How could you lose your brother?*

I ran toward the street where I'd left him. If I find him, I promised God, I'd never lose my temper again.

Bubber was sitting on the curb in front of the movie house, his arm around King. The minute he saw me he got up and walked away. "Where are you going?" I said. "Hey, aren't you going to talk?" I caught him. He pushed me away. "Didn't you ever fight before? I'm talking to you."

"Talk to yourself, Tolley. I'm not listening."

"What's that mean? You the boss now?"

"You're not my boss." He put his hands in his pockets.

"Let's go," I said.

He didn't move.

I tried to pull him. "What's the matter with you?"

"You kicked King."

"So what?"

"You hurt his feelings."

"So what? He's a dog."

"He's got feelings, too."

"What do you want me to do? Kiss him?"

"Yes. And say you're sorry."

"You say you're sorry."

Bubber grabbed me, caught my hand, bit it. I slapped him away. He went flat on his back, then he came at me again with his lips drawn back like a dog's. I backed up. He kicked at me and I stiff-armed him to keep him off. I didn't want to fight my brother. I'd never seen him like this before. He used to do anything I said.

"Say you're sorry!"

"Okay, I'm sorry, I'm sorry. Are you satisfied now?"

We walked. After a while we talked and we were friends again. I wanted to go back to the shacks, where those people were living. Maybe we could find somebody to stay with. I was tired, hungry, I needed to sleep. I thought I knew the way back, but we came out on a wide street lined with big official-looking buildings. People going in and out. On the street a crowd was gathered around a man with a monkey dressed up in a red uniform like a bellhop. The monkey was on a chain, and every time someone put a coin in his cup he raised his hat.

Shine boys were up on the steps of the court-house. There was one on every step. One of them was a woman. All of them were yelling, "Shine, shine. Five cents a shine." But she yelled the loudest. "Best shine in New York."

I watched her with a customer, a man in a black overcoat and a big hat. He looked like a judge. He put his foot on the shoe box. Big feet, too. She sat on a stool and polished with two brushes, then finished with a long polishing cloth that she whipped over the shoes. "There you are, sir." She tapped his shoes, and he dropped some money in her hand.

As soon as he was gone, she said to us, "Get out of here. You're blocking the customers."

We moved to another step. Bubber took off his aviator's hat and held it out. I stood behind him with my hand sort of raised. I had my eyes closed. I made believe that I'd been blinded during the war. Mustard gas. "You want something?" Someone gave me a stinging slap on my hand. It was the woman. "Scram," she said.

29

I was walking and dreaming, asleep on my feet. Bubber held my hand and I followed him. It was nighttime and I dreamed it was summer and I was walking in the sand in my bare feet. At Orchard Beach with my father. I wore my bathing suit under my pants. After we swam we'd go into the bushes and change.

We stopped to rest by the side of a building. Sometimes a car passed. Snow fell. It melted on the ground but stuck in Bubber's hair. It came slanting into us. My feet were wet and I felt the water squishing in my shoes. Around me, everything was moving, the wind, the cars, the snow. I kept walking . . . walking . . . sleeping . . .

I slept over a warm grate. King licked my face.

"Tolley!" Bubber shook me awake. He looked like a snowman. He pulled me up.

The snow had stopped. We were on a broad

avenue, lit up, bright and empty. The snow glittered and the apartment buildings were white and still. We were the only people on the street. A dead street, and we were dead, too. Everything seemed to come from far away. My head hurt. Nothing looked right. An approaching car's lights came at me like huge cat's eyes, the bumper full of shiny teeth. And on the roofs I saw gargoyles and gorillas jumping up and down.

We stood under a long green awning out of the snow, then went inside the building. A uniformed doorman chased us out. We went into another building. I rested my hands on top of the radiator and pushed my feet underneath till my shoes started to burn. Then Bubber heard someone and pushed me out. I shook; my teeth were chattering. I walked with my eyes closed, holding on to Bubber's arm.

"Bubber, my big little brother." He led and I followed. "You be the daddy." I talked silly. My lips felt puffy. My voice sounded funny. "You be the big brother and I'll be the little brother." We were playing together in the living room. My mother was by the stove. I rolled on the round hassock. Then Bubber sat on my back. I was the horse and he was the cowboy. The bad guy was hiding behind the chair. "Behind the chair," Bubber yelled, and kicked me in the ribs.

Later, down behind buildings in the empty lots

we saw men standing around a fire. Sparks shot up in the air. "Hey, you kids, what have you got?"

King growled. Bubber pushed me ahead of him into the dark. We crawled into a pipe to get out of the wind, but it was too cold. We walked again.

We found a broken couch leaning against a building. It was covered by a canvas that we pulled over us. We slept there. Once I woke, damp, sweating, water spilling out of me.

I woke with the sun in my eyes. The snow melted and dripped off trees and wires. King barked at an orange cat on top of a rusted iron can. A man came out of the house, yelling at King. "Go on. Scat. Git!"

We jumped up. I was dizzy for a second and then we ran.

30

We walked slowly along the Concourse. My legs felt weak. Every couple of steps I stopped to rest. The streets were crowded with shoppers. It was cold, the sun was high, people hurried into stores, or waited for buses, or sat in restaurants or at lunch counters. We walked again. I was coughing and sniffling and looking at my hands. I was dirty and ashamed.

"Tolley," Bubber said, "you all right?"

I coughed. I felt awful. I had to sit down. I couldn't get the cough out of my chest. "People are looking at me," I said.

"No, they're not."

I sat on the curb, leaned against a pole. I closed my eyes.

King licked my face. Bubber tried to pull me up. He wouldn't leave me alone. "You're sick, Tolley. Momma puts us in bed when we're sick."

My eyes started to close. I started to dream about my own bed, my room, the door shut.

Bubber shook me. "Tolley!" He pulled me to my feet. "We're going home."

"We can't . . . You can't . . ." I knocked into him. I was rolling around. I couldn't stay on my feet. "McKenzie's there."

"If we see him we'll run away." Bubber took me home. He held my arm and made me walk down Fordham Road. We turned on Webster Avenue. King ran into me. Bubber never let me stop. We walked under the Third Avenue el, getting closer and closer to home.

It was dark when we stood across the street from our apartment. We entered the courtyard on the park side. Nobody saw us. But King wouldn't go inside with us. He squirmed out of Bubber's hands and hid in the bushes.

"Okay, stay," Bubber said. "Stay. Good dog."

We went up the stairs. Every sound made my stomach jump. Bubber took my key and unlocked the door. We tiptoed through the unlit apartment. I was home. I smelled the furniture and clean linen. Were we really home? Could we stay? Everything scared me. Why was the closet door open? Why was the bed unmade? Had I left it that way? The note I'd written my parents was on the table in the hall. Was that where I'd left it?

In the other room the chairs pulled out from the table looked at me accusingly. Where have you been? Look at you. What have you been doing? You can't sit on us with those clothes on.

Bubber walked slowly to his bed and pulled out the box of toys from underneath and looked at it, then pushed it back under. He switched the light off and on and pulled down the shades and let them snap up.

In the bathroom I leaned over the sink. The soap had melted. The sink smiled up at me. The mirror said comb your hair.

I washed my hands and face and combed my hair. Then I undressed and got into bed. Bubber brought me hot water in a cup and half a Baby Ruth he had saved.

A noise, a buzzer woke me. Startled me. I sat up. I was so scared I couldn't speak. Bubber sat up. He had been asleep at the foot of my bed. Somebody was coming up the stairs. I heard the footsteps, wondered, as I always did, man or woman? Girl or boy?

The steps reached our landing and paused. Was it somebody for us? Or the Chrissmans? The steps started again on the next flight of stairs.

The house was waking up. I heard radios and water running and smelled coffee and eggs. The same old familiar sounds. Nothing had changed. Only us.

31

Bubber went downstairs to find King. I stayed in bed and waited for him. He came back alone. "King is gone."

"Maybe he went back to the cave," I said. "He could be waiting for us there, right now."

Bubber shook his head.

"He's around," I said. "He has to be." Bubber didn't say anything. "Look, he can take care of himself. He did it before us. He can do it again."

My brother just looked at me, like he knew something I didn't know. "King's not coming back."

I slept. Bubber went out and came back with Drake's cakes and an orange. I got up and dressed. My throat hurt but my chest felt better. "You want to go look for King?"

Bubber shook his head.

We went up the stairs to the landing by the door to the roof. It was safer here. "You want to go back to the cave and look?" Bubber shook his head. He wasn't looking anymore. He didn't even want to talk about King. The dog had gone around the corner and disappeared.

"I see Daddy's hand," Bubber said later. He was leaning on the railing, looking down the stairwell.

I heard somebody coming slowly up the stairs. "It's not Daddy! Let's get out of here."

"I see Daddy's hand," Bubber said again.

I looked. There was a hand on the railing below. "It's somebody else," I said.

"I'm going down."

I was afraid it was McKenzie. I made a grab for him, but he had already started down the stairs.

32

My father was down on one knee holding Bubber in his arms and kissing him. Bubber was crying. My father was crying, too. I just stood there. I didn't cry. I didn't do anything. I didn't move.

In the apartment, my father turned to me. "Well?" He held his arms out to me. He wanted me to come, but I couldn't make myself go to him.

"Come here," my father said. "You're so thin. What have you been eating? Where were you? I've been looking for you everywhere. Nobody saw you. Nobody knew where you were. It was like the ground swallowed you up."

I couldn't speak.

He took hold of me. "What's the matter with you? You don't act glad to see your father."

I ducked away from him. "Leave me alone." When he tried to pull me back, I knocked his hand away. I hit him. I hit my father. I was crazy. "Where have you been?" I was so mad I yelled at him. I didn't care what I said. "We were sick. Bubber was sick. We didn't have any money. Where were you? Why did you stay away so long? You didn't write. I wrote you and you never answered. You left us. You forgot about us. Didn't you know? Didn't you know? How could you be so dumb?"

I bit my lip. I wasn't going to let myself cry. *No crying*. I held my breath. I started coughing and crying. My father got hold of me and I burrowed my head against him, dug in, held on to him. I was bawling and hitting my head against him and wiping my tears on his shirt.

"A good boy," my father said. "A good boy."

Later we got dressed and went out to eat. My father taped the soles of my shoes with adhesive. "Tomorrow we'll go to Thom McAn and buy you both shoes."

In the cafeteria my father watched us eat. He went back and got us seconds. I worried that he didn't have enough money. "Eat. Let me worry about the money."

On the way back to the house, my father told us about being away. He had found a little work in Washington, not a lot, not enough. "Things were no different from New York. It was worse than here because I was alone. I missed you. I wrote from Washington, and when I didn't get an answer, not one letter from Momma, I got worried and I called a friend. He called me back and said Momma was in the hospital. He didn't know where you were."

"They wouldn't let us see her." Bubber's face filled.

My father held Bubber in his lap and gave a long sigh. I felt something catch in my throat. "Momma's very sick," he said. "They sent her away to a sanatorium."

"Is she going to die?" Bubber said.

"In the mountains, Momma will have fresh air. She'll eat, she'll sleep, she'll get better."

"Buba?" I said.

"She was in the hospital, too. Now she's home. Tomorrow the three of us will go see her."

33

Bubber and I are back in school again. My mother isn't home yet. My father's working downtown. The city is renovating a bunch of theaters and music halls. Maybe you think that's crazy, spending money on shows when people are hungry, but it's giving a lot of people work. Carpenters, painters, electricians, and actors and musicians, too. My father says the job is going to last a year, at least. He's redoing the gold work and says it's a job for a fly. I went down to see him one day. The inside of the theater is like a church. My father was working on the ceiling. I didn't see him at first. Then my eyes went up the scaffolding, up, up, up, and there was my father, all the way on top.

Bubber still has trouble with his words, still reads things backward and sometimes writes them that way, too. He says he's okay, he's reading. What he's doing is faking it better, guessing and listening hard.

At night, if my father's late coming home, Bubber and I go out and wait by the station.

I missed a whole civics unit. The teacher said I'd have to read the pages on my own and answer the questions because it was going to be on the final test. I had stuff to make up in algebra and spelling (I missed a lot of words), and I have to write a composition about an imaginary adventure. I thought I'd write about being hungry and finding food in garbage cans, except nobody would believe it. It's queer being here, at home and in school, and remembering how we lived under the burned-out restaurant. And then I think about the night we slept in a box, and I think of my grandmother, sick and all alone, and it makes me feel really bad.

Nobody knows about what happened to us or where we were. I don't talk about it. It didn't happen to them, and I don't want to hear people making stupid remarks like the only hungry people are too dumb or too lazy to work. I guess that's why I won't write about it, either.

My friends sort of guess something happened to me. Once we went by the restaurant and I said, "What if there was a secret room under there? Someplace you could live that nobody knew about."

"Is that where you were?" George said.

"That's right."

"That's right! Listen to him. I thought you said you were with your parents."

"That's right, we were on vacation."

"You change your story every minute. Where'd you go?"

"Florida. We traveled around a lot."

Irv sort of knew, though. "You really lived down there? Why didn't you come to my house?"

What would they have done? Maybe let us stay. Maybe split us up. Maybe sent us to the shelter. There were too many things to explain, so I kept it to myself. Bubber and I talk sometimes about the way it was. He still misses King.

My father had a lot of questions, too. Why did I do this? Why did I do that? He didn't think I had to do things the way I did them. Mr. McKenzie would have taken care of us. I didn't answer my father. I didn't talk back, not out loud anyway. Before, I never even *thought* back to him. Whatever he said was the way it was. But to myself, now, I said: *You don't know, Pop. You weren't there, so how do you know what I should have done?*

I'm delivering papers door to door in the mornings before school. I've got the money for Mr. Lazinski for the doughnuts. As soon as I get up the nerve to face him, I'm going to go down there and pay him back.

151

On my paper route, sometimes the only person I see that early in the morning is the milkman. We meet on the stairs, or going over the roof to the next building. He's friendly. He calls me Tolley and I call him Mike. I always give him a paper. He wants to pay me but I don't let him.

We went to see my mother in Tupper Lake. It's an all-day trip by train up to the Adirondacks, almost to Canada. Tupper Lake is in the mountains, but it's flat where the sanatorium is. The mountains are all around it. My mother took a walk with us. She held Bubber's hand the whole time. She held my hand, too.

I didn't like going away and leaving her again, leaving her in the mountains. I didn't like those cold white mountains. They say there are bears in the mountains, and wolves and mountain lions. I don't like to think about Bubber and me alone out there. I feel a lot safer in the city.